## A COLD BLOODED KILLER

Lassiter swung in close and brought the butt of his knife down hard on Joplin's right wrist. Joplin gave a yelp of pain and dropped his knife. It lay glittering in the dust. Before he could retrieve it, however, the knife was covered by Lassiter's foot.

A gasp went up from the crowd as Lassiter said, "By rights I could kill you."

"You ain't got the guts."

"You're right. I couldn't kill you in cold blood as you did Timmie Borling."

It brought an exclamation from the onlookers because most of them were unaware of Joplin's hand in Borling's death.

Drawing back his foot, Lassiter kicked the knife across the ground into the crowd. Then he threw his own knife after it.

"We'll finish as we started it," Lassiter snarled, lifting his fists...

Other *Leisure* books by Loren Zane Grey:

**LASSITER**

# LOREN ZANE GREY

## AMBUSH FOR LASSITER

LEISURE BOOKS     NEW YORK CITY

A LEISURE BOOK®

June 2005

Published by special arrangement with Golden West Literary Agency.

Dorchester Publishing Co., Inc.
200 Madison Avenue
New York, NY 10016

ISBN 0-8439-5419-1

The name "Leisure Books" and the stylized "L" with design are trademarks of Dorchester Publishing Co., Inc.

Printed in the United States of America.

# AMBUSH FOR LASSITER

# Chapter One

Lassiter's dark face was somber as he listened to his cellmate, Timmie Borling, explain. Even though it seemed a fairly simple plan, with minimum risks, Lassiter was still on edge. According to Borling, Joplin, the head guard, was to be bribed. A pretty girl who worked in a cantina in the village below the prison was to hide the bribe money where Borling could find it and turn it over to the head guard.

"There's something wrong with the plan," Lassiter hissed, glancing, through the bars and across a narrow corridor to another cell, making sure they weren't overheard.

Borling's handsome face reflected impatience. "Nothin's wrong, Lassiter."

"Then tell me, who's furnishing the bribe money?" Lassiter asked skeptically.

"The gal don't know. But it's gotta be some unknown friend who knows damn well we ain't guilty."

Lassiter swore softly. In his faded prison denims he looked taller than his five foot eleven inches. Strong

1

shoulders tapered to a narrow waist and his legs were long and powerful. "Who's this unknown friend? That's what I want to know."

The big sandy-haired Borling made an impatient gesture. "Could be anybody, damn it."

"It makes me wonder, Timmie. Joplin letting us work away from the others for five days in a row. Then this girl just happening by and taking a shine to you. . . ."

"I'm a good-lookin' fella." Borling winked and strutted down the narrow cell, his thumbs under his armpits. Then he halted, abruptly serious. "I'm takin' this gamble mainly for my boy. I've got a feelin' in my gut that Rance needs me."

Lassiter swallowed. "Escape, yeah, I agree to that. I just don't like Joplin's hand in it."

"He's got an itch for money. That's why it'll work." Borling gripped Lassiter's shoulder. "You with me?"

Lassiter nodded.

The following morning they were marched down from the prison along with eight other convicts, through a brushy stretch along the river and to the cotton fields with only the head guard Joplin to watch over them.

Once there, Borling counted off seven paces of a man's long stride, which meant fourteen of a woman's shorter steps. It led into a great tangle of mesquite. Beyond that was the river, dazzling in the early sun. Lassiter saw Borling kneel before a large flat rock and start to dig.

"By God, she did it, Lassiter," Borling said fiercely after a few minutes. He lifted his dirt-encrusted hands,

2

which held gold pieces he had scooped from their hiding place.

Lassiter's heartbeat quickened as he stared at the shining gold coins. A glance through the mesquite showed the heavyset head guard, Meager Joplin, plodding toward them, with a rifle under his thick arm.

This was Lassiter's cue to get to work. He began to whack the ground with his short-handled hoe, keeping one eye on Borling, who was slowly straightening up. Joplin drew near, a scowl on his broad, savage face.

Joplin came to a halt, looking carefully over his shoulder at the eight other convicts working the cotton patch some distance away. "You got the money?" he demanded of Borling. This prompted Borling to open both large hands so Joplin could see the fifty glittering double eagles. Without a word they were eagerly snatched by Joplin and sent jingling into his pants pockets.

"Get goin', you two," he hissed and his eyes swung to Lassiter. Then he was striding back toward the patch where the others were working.

"I don't trust Joplin," Lassiter said in a low voice, grabbing Borling by an arm.

But Borling shook free, his teeth gleaming. "Forget that ! It worked. I knew it would."

Stooping, he picked up his chain, a three-foot spread of links between each ankle that was locked with a band of steel. He pushed deeper into the mesquite. Only for a few seconds did Lassiter tarry, then he picked up his own chain and hurried after Borling, who by now was some fifteen feet ahead.

Mesquite offered a perfect screen as, bent low, they

put some distance between themselves and the other convicts. At each step, when there was no alarm, Lassiter began to take heart. He was not breathing hard from the exertion, for in the eight months he and Borling had been confined to Rimshaw Prison, he had kept himself in shape. Holding the chain with one hand, thrusting aside mesquite with the other, Lassiter was dimly aware of hoofbeats.

The sudden sound of a rifle exploded the morning stillness. Lassiter turned cold as he saw Borling, ahead of him, suddenly stagger. A small wet spot appeared on the left side of his back. Borling's face was already beginning to collapse as he looked around at Lassiter. His eyes reflected physical pain as well as the realization of betrayal.

"Tell Delira . . ." It was all Borling managed to say as his lips suddenly bubbled red and he fell to his knees, then over on his side.

A second rifle shot exploded through mesquite, clipping branches as Lassiter was frozen in his hunched-over position. One branch struck him hard on the forehead, breaking the skin. The next bullet, Lassiter knew instinctively, would be for him, dead center. Knowing there was nothing he could do now for Timmie Borling, he bared his teeth, leaped over the body and began a clanking run, with a snarl of defiance on his sun-darkened features. Where the mesquite thinned he could see vague running figures with rifles coming down from the prison. At that moment Joplin spotted him, coming at a dead run while Lassiter was hampered by the leg chain.

Joplin halted and lifted his rifle. But in those seconds there was a shout as a tall, harassed-looking man astride a buckskin came pounding up.

"Hold it, Joplin!" the rider said, brandishing a pistol. It was Seymour Galendor, superintendent of Rimshaw Prison. Pulling in the buckskin in a spray of sand, he pointed his pistol at Lassiter.

At first, a panting Lassiter thought Galendor was in on it. But he quickly changed his mind upon seeing a look of mingled rage and concern on Joplin's broad face.

"I'll handle this tough one, Mr. Galendor," Joplin snarled. Joplin lunged but Galendor spurred the horse just a second later. The flank of the horse bumped Joplin, thus saving Lassiter from having his skull smashed in by the butt plate of the man's rifle, which was truly Joplin's intent. Even so, the heavy stock of the weapon struck him solidly on the jaw. Everything crumbled into blackness.

Galendor looked regretfully down at Lassiter. "Lassiter, I'm truly disappointed. I allowed you and your friend Borling to be on this detail because I felt sorry for you. And you repay me by trying to escape."

His speech was wasted because Lassiter was out of it.

"I had a hunch I'd have trouble from these two," Joplin said, giving the superintendent a narrow sidelong glance. "Lucky I seen 'em tryin' to get away."

Galendor, a slender man in his forties, put his attention thoughtfully on Joplin. "I want Lassiter *alive*." He stared into the yellowish eyes of the head guard. "You understand, Joplin?"

"Yes, sir."

Galendor gave a long sigh. "I suppose Lassiter will have to be dealt with in the usual manner. As an example to the other prisoners." He seemed saddened. From the first, it had been thought in many quarters that Galendor was far too sensitive a person to run a tough prison such as Rimshaw. He had received his appointment as prison superintendent from the territorial governor, who happened to be his brother-in-law.

"It should be enough punishment, the fact that his friend was killed," Galendor said with a shake of his head. "But unfortunately it isn't."

At first, when Lassiter finally opened his eyes and saw nothing but blackness, he wondered if this was death and would he soon be joining the late Timmie Borling? Then he placed the palms of both hands down on a flat surface and felt cold stone.

Although in his eight months at Rimshaw Prison he had never been in this room before, he knew instinctively what it was.

The hole!

He was sitting on the floor, back against a wall. He wondered how long he had been unconscious. Lassiter had no memory of being brought here. Working his jaw, he felt pain. It bore a deep cut from the stock of Joplin's rifle.

Just thinking about Joplin knotted his stomach. By that alone he knew he was alive and not dead; he doubted that the dead were consumed by such a rage as now gripped him.

To Lassiter, time crawled as if burdened by heavy chains. Twice a day he was fed when a tin plate and cup were slid into his cell through an opening at the bottom of the door. Most of the time he didn't know whether the tepid water and stale bread was breakfast or supper. On alternate days he was fed a watery stew.

One day the door opened. Light flooded the cell like a blow across Lassiter's eyes after living in darkness. It was the superintendent, Galendor, who spoke.

"Don't get up from the floor," he warned nervously. "If you do, I'll shoot."

"What do you want?" Lassiter asked bitterly.

"Tell me about Joplin's part in your attempted escape."

Lassiter thought about it a moment. Believing it might be a trap and that Joplin would beat him half to death with his club, he only shrugged and said nothing.

Galendor looked exasperated. His brown hair was thinning. As usual there was a harassed look about him, as if he had been thrust into a job that over-reached his capabilities. "Tell me, Lassiter," he urged. "You know what I mean."

Lassiter considered telling him about the girl who, according to Borling, worked in a cantina in the village of Rimshaw. Had she been part of the plot, or simply a go-between whose only crime had been to hide the money? She had appeared almost miraculously the second day after Timmie Borling and Lassiter had been assigned to the cotton field.

That day Lassiter had been sent by Joplin to sharpen tools. So Timmie Borling got to her first. They struck up a conversation. If Joplin noticed it, he paid no attention. She came by each day, a slender, dark-haired girl, waving to Lassiter from a distance, then talking a few minutes with Borling. Joplin always seemed to be at the other end of the field when the girl appeared, Lassiter recalled.

"Money was left for us," Lassiter said thinly when he thought of the useless death of his friend.

"Who left the money, Lassiter?"

"I'd rather not say." He fully intended to escape, one way or another, at which time he'd ask his own questions. He looked up at Galendor in the doorway in a gray suit that fit him loosely, attesting to the fact that he had lost weight since taking the prison job. His right hand was clamped to the butt of a holstered revolver.

"It was Joplin's suggestion that you and Borling be put in the cotton field," Galendor said wearily. "I followed his lead as he'd been here longer than I. I'm talking about money which was used to bribe Joplin. I finally put the loose ends together. The so-called bribe was Joplin's payment for turning his back while you escaped. Only to be murdered."

"Somebody wanted us dead," Lassiter said in a hard voice. A name simmered far back in his consciousness, Borling's wife Delira. She might have her faults but was she capable of such conniving?

"Anyway," Galendor was saying, "I believe my timely arrival that day saved you. Or you'd be dead along with Borling."

"I believe it."

"You're a bitter man, Lassiter, and I can't say I blame you." Galendor added, "By the way, Joplin is no longer with the prison. I fired him."

Lassiter made no comment. What was the use? The damage was done. Timmie Borling was dead.

Lassiter ran his fingers through his uncut black hair that hung far down the back of his neck. During his stay in the hole, the lower half of his face had gradually been covered with a ragged black beard.

He filled his lungs with the clear air that flowed through the doorway; the air in the cell was fetid. He thought of jumping Galendor, but knew he could never get away with it. No, he'd bide his time and plan carefully. There was a way—there *had* to be—of getting out of this place. A new harshness touched his dark eye and his hatred was like a cold knife in the heart.

Galendor said, "I'd warn you against Joplin if you were going to be free any time soon. But you have over twenty-four years to serve. And by that time I assume you both will have lost your venom." He started to close the door. "I was wrong. I said you'd be out in a little over twenty-four years. I'm sorry to say that five years will automatically be added to your sentence for the attempted escape."

# Chapter Two

Some weeks later a concerned Craig Moran rode all the way out to the north Muleshoe line shack to see the two men who had been assigned to one post. Yesterday he had heard disturbing news in Hopeville concerning a man named Bert Stencoe. It was hard to believe what he had heard and yet . . . the doubt prompted the long ride out to the line shack

Stencoe had been a nester who had been allowed by Timmie Borling to run a few head of beef on Muleshoe property. But once Borling was sent to prison and Moran had moved in as Mrs. Borling's foreman, he decided to tighten up some loose ends. One of those was Stencoe. Moran warned him about rustling Muleshoe beef and selling it across the mountain. Although Moran had no proof, he knew damn well Stencoe was a rustler. He had words with him one day in town.

"Timmie Borling always let me have my own way," Stencoe had stated flatly. "What I'm doin' is the only way I can fight back against the ones that done him in."

Moran felt himself stiffen as Stencoe looked him right in the eye. Now what the hell did that mean? Moran wondered. And just how much did Stencoe know? Mainly about the death of Dave Ashburn. He had felt sure that with the local people agitated over the cold-blooded killing that Borling and Lassiter would get the gallows. They hadn't and it was a disappointment.

And now on this warm day he could see the line shack ahead at Rubio Springs—a mere dot at the foot of a towering red cliff. After hiring them earlier in the year, Moran had assigned the Sagar brothers to the line shack. They seldom came to town. A vicious pair, the brothers, with loyalty only to themselves. He found them moving cattle out of a valley to better grass.

They seemed surprised to see him at the lonely outpost and pulled up their horses and waited for him to speak.

Moran came right to the point. "I told you boys to hang Bert Stencoe to his own porch. You said you did it."

The bushy-browed Rupe, a year older than his brother Petey, said, "We hung him high just like you said."

"You sure?"

"Hell, we stayed around till he stopped twitchin'," Petey put in with a laugh.

Rupe's right cheek bulged with tobacco. He leaned over to spit on an anthill, which created a frenzied colony as ants were inundated by a brown ocean of tobacco juice. "How come you don't believe us?" Rupe Sagar fixed Moran with a cold eye.

"Something's come up. There are people who claim he didn't die that way. That he took a shotgun and blew off his head."

"He was dead as last Christmas at the end of the rope we hung him with," Rupe Sagar said heavily. "Any head-blowin' with a shotgun, somebody else done it, not him."

Moran felt a wall of animosity stream from the brothers and he made waving motions with his hands. "I take your word for it, boys. Somebody's been playing games that I don't like."

Two days later in town, Moran had just ridden in from Muleshoe when the northbound stage pulled up in front of the hotel. He was a tall, ruggedly built man whose exceptionally handsome features were somewhat spoiled by a nose once broken and not properly set. Women said it gave him a certain devilish charm. He believed them.

He was about to skirt the tail end of the stage when the single passenger alighted to the walk. Moran caught his breath. In the southern part of the territory—Rimshaw village to be exact—he'd had a conversation with the man, who was oversized with a rope of lank brown hair hanging across a low forehead. Moran picked up the pace he had started at the sight of Joplin but the man called to him.

"Moran. Craig Moran."

A tremor traveled across Moran's shoulder blades. How the hell did he learn my name? was the thought that screamed through his head. Down at Rimshaw he had played a role and covered his tracks well. Or so he had thought.

"You spoke to me?" Moran asked coldly. Joplin couldn't possibly have recognized him.

"No use us tryin' to fool each other, Moran," Joplin said in a gravelly voice. His smile exposed a row of stained teeth.

"I'm afraid there's been some mistake." With a whoop and crack of whip from its driver, the stage-coach lurched into movement, heading for the north road out of town.

"I worked two years with a medicine show," Joplin said with a tight smile. "Jack Peeples always wore a bushy beard when he was doin' his show. Afterwards he took it off."

"So?"

"So if anybody started chasin' us outta town we could say there was no bearded gent with us. We'd say the bearded fella quit us an' went off somewhere else."

Moran's voice sounded icy when he said, "If I were you, I'd get out of Hopeville. . . ."

"I need a job."

Moran let down a little. So that's all Joplin wanted. He had halfway expected a try for petty blackmail.

"I had a good job," Joplin said, his voice on edge. "I lost it on account of the prison super takin' a ride the mornin' we planned the prison break. Otherwise every-thing would've been settled. Lassiter dead as well as Borling. And I'd still have a good job."

"I'm sorry about your job, but . . ."

"I can spot a false beard a block away after workin'

13

around Jack Peeples for so long." When Moran made as if to move on, Joplin caught him by the arm near the elbow with such force that Moran felt a jolt of pain. "One thing for sure, Lassiter'll keep on till he does get outta Rimshaw. An' he'll be headin' this way on account of his friend Borling bein' done in."

Joplin released his arm. Although Moran had an urge to massage away the pain, he refused to give the man that much satisfaction. Besides, what Joplin had just said was making his mind spin.

"Has what you said about Lassiter getting out of Rimshaw . . . escaping . . . got anything to do with a man named Stencoe?"

When Joplin only shrugged, Moran made up his mind. The man's powerful build might prove advantageous. At least for a time. After that, he'd get rid of him, one way or another. A breeze sprang up suddenly causing miniature tornadoes of dust to spring up along the street. Horses switched tails and dogs barked. A woman loaded down with purchases hurried from the Mercantile, her skirts billowing.

"Joplin," Moran said crisply, "you've got a job. I never should've tried to fool a man as smart as you."

A lank man with a weathered face, a star pinned to his vest, came out of the hotel. He slowed on long legs, looked Joplin over, then gave Moran a nod.

"Howdy," he said in a cool voice

"Hello, Sheriff."

As the sheriff crossed the street to the Trail's End, Moran vowed that once he was safely married to Delira Borling and had Muleshoe in his grasp, he would pull enough strings to get rid of Sheriff Jim Sloan.

Moran got Joplin a horse at the livery barn and they rode toward Muleshoe. To their left was a great rise of storm-smoothed rock topped by cracked and leaning crags. Powdery dust lifted by their horses spun into the air to hang suspended as balls of beige-colored clouds. Cedars had taken root here and there on the denuded surface. The two riders were a contrast, the well-dressed thirty-year-old Moran and the slightly older, much heaver Joplin with his brutal face.

Finally, at the entrance of a long valley, Moran pointed out the Muleshoe headquarters in the distance, dominated by a white two-story house. There were barns and outbuildings, corrals and pastures where horses grazed.

Just as they entered the yard, Delira was coming down the veranda steps. She gestured to Moran. "Craig, I want to talk to you about the schoolhouse dance. . . ." Her gaze settled on the bulky Joplin riding at Moran's side. "Who's he?" she wanted to know.

Moran swore softly but had no choice but to introduce them.

Moran took him to the big barn where they left the horses. He introduced him to hands working there. The barn smelled of dust, and spiders and mice could be heard scurrying across the loft.

At the bunkhouse, Moran pointed out an empty bunk where Joplin dumped his warbag. There was no one else in the large building. "By the way, how'd you find out who I was?"

Joplin smiled, sat on the bunk and began to work off

15

his boots. "I figured how you'd look without the beard. I never forget a face. One time you tried to sell some cows to a fella I was workin' for at the Triple-X outfit down near San Antone."

"Oh? You worked for old man Samuels?"

"Yeah. Those cows you tried to sell him had brands worked over with a runnin' iron. Kind of a botched-up job, he thought." Joplin chuckled. "But that was a long time ago, eh, *amigo?*"

Moran winced at the word *amigo*, but managed a grin. "Keep it under your hat, eh?"

"I got a permanent job?" Joplin drawled.

"Permanent," Moran said with a straight face.

"I had a good job. Head guard at the prison. Then that damn business about the escape came up and I jumped for it." Joplin looked Moran in the eye. "You put out some good bait, Moran. A thousand dollars in gold to be hid by that black-haired gal from Paco's."

Moran started for the door, not liking to be reminded of how things had gone wrong down at Rimshaw Prison. Joplin commented on the spacious bunkhouse.

"Old man Butler who started this place," Moran explained from the doorway, "wanted the best for his hired hands. Borling's first wife was his daughter."

"Then that pretty Mrs. Borling I just met ain't the first?"

"No, she isn't. I plan to marry her."

"Then you'll own it all, the whole place."

"A husband has his rights," Moran said with a shrug.

In the morning Moran hired the Sagar brothers for a special job. Anyone heading north to Hopeville from the direction of Rimshaw Prison would undoubtedly stop off at the first habitation, a place known as the Crossroads. Moran described Lassiter to Rupe and his brother Petey; he told them to hang around the place a month if necessary. There would be four hundred dollars in it for the job.

Petey Sagar wiped his nose on a shirt sleeve. "Sounds like easy money."

"From all I've heard, Lassiter's nobody to fool with," Moran warned. "He's got rattler speed in his gunhand. Just be careful."

It took two days of fast riding to reach the Crossroads. On the day of their arrival, the rambling, two-story place was busy. East- and west-bound stages had pulled in at the same time.

Lew Oliver, a wheezing fat man who owned the place, looked the Sagar brothers over, not liking what he saw.

"Don't see nobody that looks like Lassiter," Rupe grunted after scanning passengers wolfing down their food at a big table.

Oliver's sharp ear behind the bar picked up the remark. "Why do you want Lassiter?"

"He'll be comin' through here, maybe. If he does . . ."

Rupe Sagar grinned and spread his hands.

Lew Oliver said, "Lassiter's doin' twenty-five years down at Rimshaw Prison, the way I hear it. You'll have a damn long wait."

Petey Sagar gave a vicious laugh. "Roll us out two cool beers, fat man."

"I don't want you hombres hangin' around here."

Rupe, who was at the end of the bar, out of sight of

the diners, drew his gun with astounding speed and jammed the muzzle into Oliver's soft rib cage. Oliver turned pale.

"A certain fella figures Lassiter might be comin' through here," Rupe snarled softly. "We'll be stayin' till we make sure. An' you keep quiet about us lookin' for Lassiter. You hear?" Cold sweat ran down the back of Oliver's plump neck.

# Chapter Three

The days dragged on for Lassiter in the eternal darkness. He would walk, feeling his way so as not to run into a wall. When it grew hot inside he guessed it was midday. Over the days the palms of his hands became sore where he dug in his nails so as to feel pain. Pain enabled him to cling to his sanity—at times by a thread. When he had been brought to the prison they said he would soon die from fighting the heat and monotony on this bleak pile of rock and iron. And he was still fighting it.

Eight months ago, when Lassiter and Borling had been brought to Rimshaw Prison, they were told how lucky they were. Because it was unusual on the raw frontier not to exact an eye for an eye. He and Borling had escaped the hangman's noose.

Many times during his stay in the hole the botched escape plot filled his mind. A dark-eyed, pretty girl from the town below the prison out for a stroll, coming past the cotton patch where Lassiter and Borling were working. Joplin allowing them to work apart from the others in the detail, which in itself was odd. The girl supposedly taking a shine to Timmie Borling and finally making a proposition about bribery. And the payoff had been death. Timmie Borling with his final breath had uttered the name of his wife—Delira. Did that indicate that his wife, clear up in Hopeville in the northern part of the territory, had engineered the deadly business? There was no denying that she had turned her back on Borling from the moment of his arrest. She was even suing for divorce, a bold step for a wife to take in this wild country.

For the past year, Lassiter had been working with his friend Timmie Borling on the latter's Muleshoe Ranch. When Lassiter had come to work there, Borling, a widower, had been married to Delira less than a year. At first, Delira and Borling's son by his previous marriage had seemed to hit it off. But at the last, Lassiter sensed an undercurrent between the seven-year-old boy and his stepmother.

Their downfall, Borling's and Lassiter's, was a result of Borling's love of poker. Once a week there was a marathon game at a Muleshoe line shack, which was midway between the ranch and the town of Hopeville. In the final game, Dave Ashburn, who had recently taken over the town's livery barn and who considered himself a ladies' man, had been the big winner. Lassiter and Borling and Ashburn had been the final players; the others had departed.

The next morning Ashburn's body was found near town. He had been shot several times in the back. Scratched in the dust near his outstretched right hand were two names: Lassiter, Borling.

They were accused of murder, quickly tried and sentenced to twenty-five years in Rimshaw Prison.

In Lassiter's solid rock cell there was no cot, no chair, only a bucket. There were four similar cells reached by a flight of stone stairs. The door itself was so perfectly hung that no rim of daylight escaped around the edges.

Lassiter made up his mind to endure the long days and refuse to think of the bleak years that stretched ahead. He focused instead on somehow getting out of this awful place. And if in the process he was gunned down as Borling had been, then it would be a blessing.

When they finally checked on him he was told that he had served two months and sixteen days in the hole.

His door opened suddenly. The sunlight, dim as it was, struck his eyeballs like a blow. He threw his forearm across his eyes to shield them from the glare. His body tensed for he halfway expected a working over by guards with their clubs. So far, during his stay in the hole, he had been spared that punishment.

From the sound of footsteps he could tell that two men had entered the cell. Lassiter turned, lowering his arm slightly to adjust his gaze to the sunlight. Before being confined to the hole there had been times in his cell when he had cursed the heat of the sun. Now he marveled at the sight of it.

Two guards were eyeing him. "You're wanted up front," said a squat, powerfully built guard named Latham.

"Up front, why?" Lassiter heard himself ask, his voice sounding strange after the long months of silence.

"A surprise," said Latham almost reluctantly.

The days of darkness and solitude had nearly drained him of the will to resist. "It's some kind of a trick," Lassiter muttered.

"Wish it was," Latham said angrily. "It's on account of you that Joplin got the can tied to his britches. Come along!"

Lassiter followed Latham up the flight of steep stone stairs. The other guard left the door to Lassiter's cell open to air it out. The path led along a narrow corridor flanked by cells. Prisoners at their gratings called out to Lassiter. It seemed to take all of his strength to lift a hand to them. Through a barred window he could see the guard tower at the edge of the yard and the Gatling gun which in five seconds could riddle an escaping prisoner with bullets.

Lassiter walked erect in his faded clothing, his uncut black hair bouncing at the back of his neck at each laborious step. His ragged beard itched. But as he progressed down the hallway his strength began to return. He walked on damp stone, which meant that the cells had recently been wet down with a hose, a daily occurrence this time of year to ease the stifling heat. Rimshaw Prison had a reputation for aging a man five years for every one spent as a prisoner on the great stone hill. And it could kill him long before his time.

A batch of new prisoners stared in awe at the fierceness etched on Lassiter's dark face as he marched along, flanked by the two guards. Their boots thumped on damp stone. The new prisoners wanted to know who he was, and the old-timers told them.

"One of the toughest hombres in here . . . was partners with Timmie Borling. A mighty fine-lookin' fella, he was. Killed by a guard when he was tryin' to escape."

This caused Latham to snap, "Borling got what he deserved." The guard's voice shook, betraying his sympathy for Joplin, who had done the killing.

No expression crossed Lassiter's face. He didn't know exactly how it would be done, but somehow, somewhere he would make Joplin pay for the murder. And cold-blooded murder it was. Only by the grace of God am I alive and walking on these damp bricks, Lassiter thought.

He was ushered into Galendor's office. Latham and the other guard departed, leaving him alone.

Neatly stacked piles of paper were at each of Galendor's elbows where he sat stiffly behind a long table used as a desk. For a few moments he studied Lassiter with tired eyes, then waved him to a chair. A tall clock in a corner of the office ticked away the seconds. One wall was taken up by shelves of books, Galendor's library.

Through a barred window, Lassiter saw the hills crowned with clumps of cactus and mesquite. Birds, which looked like moving ink spots, dotted the sky. Smoke curled up from chimneys of brick or tin from the village below the prison.

"You still had a month left to serve in the hole," Galendor reminded Lassiter with a tired smile.

"I couldn't keep track of time." The sound of his own voice still seemed strange to his ears; he had been so long wrapped in silence. His gaze remained on the country he could see beyond the window. He had always considered this stretch to be the bleakest in the territory. A place to tarry only long enough for a cool beer before pushing on to more habitable climes. But today it seemed almost beautiful; the way the sun put a sheen over brush clumps and cactus and on the flats below buildings of the village.

"Over two months in the hole is harsh punishment," Galendor was saying a little sadly. Patches of sweat could be seen through the thinning hair on his narrow skull. "I guess from the first there was some doubt about your guilt, yours and Borlings."

Lassiter marveled at the scent of clean air as contrasted to the stench of unwashed bodies in the prison. He gave a short laugh. "Doubt? So they send us here to rot!"

"As a result of the doubt, leniency was shown to you."

"Tell me how." Lassiter's gaze darted to Galendor's harassed features.

"If you had climbed the thirteen steps to the gallows, it would be impossible to rectify a . . . a mistake."

Lassiter stiffened in his chair, not quite sure if he had heard the prison superintendent correctly. From the direction of the kitchen came a faint rattle of pots and pans and the booming voice of Big Sam Kearns, one of the cooks: "Prayin' for the day I lay eyes again on my Daisy Lou. . . ." Not for twenty more years would Big Sam lay eyes on his Daisy Lou.

"At least he can sing and hope, which is more than can be said for most of us here," Lassiter put in.

"He'll be dead long before his sentence is up."

I'll get out, Galendor, Lassiter wanted to shout. Somehow I'll make it. He ground his teeth to keep from uttering the threat aloud. But even as the words charged silently across his mind he faced up to reality. Very few had escaped in the dozen years Rimshaw had been in operation. Rewards, it was said, were paid for the return of those few who had, brought back to the prison in gunnysacks.

"I mentioned a mistake," Galendor said with a weary smile. "Or are you so filled with hatred that you close your ears to someone who is trying to bring you good tidings?"

"I know the game," Lassiter said roughly, the skin stretched tightly over his prominent cheekbones. "Let me out of the hole, get my hopes up, then slam the door in my face again!"

"Get a grip on yourself, man!"

"Twenty times a day I hear Timmie Borling getting gunned down and you say get a grip on yourself. . . ."

The rebuke brought a rush of color to Galendor's gaunt face. "Do you remember a man named Stencoe?"

"Had a chip on his shoulder most of the time. What's Bert Stencoe got to do with all this?"

"He confessed."

"Confessed to what?"

"That he murdered Dave Ashburn. That you and Borling are innocent."

It was as if Lassiter had been struck a savage blow in the stomach. He stared in disbelief at the prison superintendent, then sagged back in the chair, his mind spinning.

"Stencoe's *here?*"

Galendor shook his head. "I'm sorry to say . . ."

"I tried to tell 'em we were innocent! Shouted it . . ."

"After Stencoe wrote out a confession, he shot himself."

It took Lassiter a few seconds to grasp it. "A suicide? *Stencoe?*" Lassiter gripped the arms of his chair so hard that the knuckles turned white as bone. After he had gotten hold of himself, he said, "Stencoe didn't seem the kind to shoot himself."

"Well, he did."

Lassiter decided he'd already said too much, doubting openly that Stencoe would kill himself. The placid, brushy hills he could see through the window swam before his eyes, then steadied.

"I thought you'd jump up and click your heels together," Galendor said. "But you seem to be taking it very coolly."

"I'm all torn up inside," Lassiter responded in a dead voice. "Because if what you say is true, Timmie Borling died for nothing."

Galendor stared at the hard, bearded face, seeing the bright hatred in the eyes, the twist of lips. "What I'm trying to say is that you're a free man."

"I see. . . ."

"In some ways I regret turning you loose."

"Why?"

"Because you're overflowing with hatred and will undoubtedly come to no good . . ."

"It's not your worry."

". . . and take others with you."

"Anybody I take will deserve it."

Galendor folded his hands at the edge of the desk. "May I offer a suggestion?"

"Go ahead."

"Don't go back to Hopeville. Head farther north instead."

"North, why?"

"You know the cattle business. There'll be plenty of opportunities in Montana and Wyoming."

"I want to see Borling's son."

"I advise against it."

"He worried about the boy. I want to make sure he's all right."

"Next time you might not be as fortunate," Galendor pointed out. "You could get a tough jury and a tougher judge and be hanged."

Now that the prospect of freedom was gradually filtering into his consciousness, Lassiter felt his knees tremble. It was partly a reaction to the days of confinement in the hole without communication with another human being. Try as he might, he couldn't direct his hatred against the balding man who sat tensely behind a desk.

"You won't send me out of here unarmed, of course," Lassiter said quietly.

"It's against my better judgement to return your gun. But I'm obligated to do so."

From a small storeroom at the far side of the office, he produced a box. It bore Lassiter's name and contained the clothing he had worn, including his boots and hat. But no gun.

Galendor said, "Go get yourself a bath and put on clean clothes. You'll feel better. And reflect on what I've been telling you."

Lassiter stood with his clothing under one arm. "My gun," he said.

27

"Come back for it."

Latham escorted him to a room where several zinc tubs were lined up. There Lassiter sat in one of them and contemplated his future. He still wasn't completely sure that this so-called freedom wasn't a trick of some kind. But to what purpose he couldn't imagine. Unless it was to break his spirit—offer the dream of all convicts—freedom. Then yank it away.

He shaved off his beard, his hand shaking so that he nicked himself in numerous places. His cheeks grew raw from the scrape of the razor. When he was finished, Latham escorted him back to Galendor's office.

The superintendent gave him his holstered gun and belt. "In some ways I feel I'm turning loose a potential killer."

"No, you're not."

"You have that reputation in some quarters."

"The only men I've ever killed was to save my own neck. It was me or them."

Galendor gave him two double eagles. "The usual forty dollars to start a convict on his way." Then Galendor's face brightened. "But the territorial governor saw to it that you were to be given a bonus. One hundred dollars extra for suffering false imprisonment."

It was an effort for Lassiter to fight down harsh laughter and an urge to hurl the coins in Galendor's face. Yet he couldn't blame the man; he was only carrying out orders.

Lassiter dropped the coins into his pocket. "Am I free to go?"

Galendor said, "All I can do now is wish you luck." He offered his hand. They shook.

Latham escorted Lassiter to the main gate where he quickly signed some papers. Not many weeks before, Latham had used his club on Lassiter's ribs because of an imagined infraction of prison rules.

"Maybe it's a good thing Borling never lived to see this day," Latham said smugly.

Lassiter turned on him. "Why'd you say that?"

"Because he'd see another man in his wife's bedroom. An' he might lose his head. Then he'd be back in here again. Either that or hung. I hear she's a pretty woman. Killin' one of 'em can make a judge an' jury powerful mad."

Lassiter kept a checkrein on his temper.

Latham pressed on, grinning. "Seems that Borling couldn't keep his woman. Seems that she found a better man."

Lassiter turned his back on the stocky guard and stepped through the gate. It closed at his back. Lassiter took a moment to buckle his gun belt, with Latham watching him through the bars of the gate.

"Ain't no shells in it, Lassiter," Latham taunted. "None at your belt, either. In case you're wishin' to blow me outta my boots."

Lassiter didn't bother to reply, but started walking down the hill in the hot sun. In the space of little over an hour he had been confined in the hole and here he was a free man. He took a deep breath of the clear air, smelling the sage, the dust, the wild things.

It was on this day that the Sagar brothers, Rupe and Petey, started their vigil at the Crossroads far to the north on the approach to Hopeville.

# Chapter Four

After a few steps on the steep road, Lassiter felt dizzy from all those weeks of inactivity in solitary confinement. Near the river below, the flat-roofed buildings of the village of Rimshaw swam in the heat. He lurched on, feeling worse than drunk, his heart pounding, drops of sweat dancing along his brow at each labored step. It was almost like coming out of a drunk, wondering where you had spent the night. But he knew where he had spent the night—many of them—in a dungeon of the prison high above the town on a rocky hill.

Finally, he was in the town and on a plank walk. His feet hurt in the boots with built-up heels, because for months he had walked in flat heels. He halted, looking around, jerking his hat brim to cut the brassy sunlight. There wasn't much to the place, only one street with a few buildings and behind it some residences spaced up a steep hillside. In front was the dazzling river with a smear of smoke from a steamer. There were only a few people on the walk. A glance at the sun told him it was midday. His rumbling stomach announced its needs. For breakfast that morning it had been the usual stale bread and water.

Down the street he saw a sign: PACO'S. GAMES. WHISKEY. His eyes burned as he stared at it, recalling Timmie Borling saying that the girl who would help get them free was named Felicia and that she worked at a place in Rimshaw called Paco's. It all came back to him in a rush.

Lassiter had seen her only from a distance. A female Judas she had turned out to be.

The smell of cooking food caused him to turn and locate the source. In a small cafe he sat with his back to the wall. There were only two other diners, cowboys from the looks of them. A strong odor of stale grease and tobacco smoke hovered in the air. A fat waiter waddled over to Lassiter's table. His bushy brows lifted slightly at the size of Lassiter's order.

"I've heard of a fella bein' hungry enough to eat a mule," the waiter said with a faint laugh. Then he barked the order at a perspiring cook who worked at a big stove.

After putting away a huge steak, a double order of beans and fried potatoes and two slices of dried apple pie, Lassiter patted his full stomach.

When he paid for his meal, the waiter said, "You just passin' through, stranger?"

"Been delayed a few months," Lassiter replied with a bitter laugh and rolled his eyes upward toward the prison on the hill.

The waiter looked at him closer. "Rimshaw Prison?" Lassiter nodded and the waiter said, "Friend of mine was up there and had five years to do. But he never lasted much past the first one. A tough place."

"I'm sitting here courtesy of a man named Stencoe," Lassiter said through thin lips. "I figure he's the biggest damn liar ever put on God's green earth."

The waiter, not knowing what he meant, blinked and walked away.

At a general store, Lassiter purchased shells for his gun and belt. Only when the weapon was loaded, and the shell belt filled did he feel like a whole man. With a hundred and five dollars jingling in his pocket, he went to a livery stable and dickered for a horse. Finally, he settled on a roan for fifty dollars, with a saddle thrown in. Not much of a mount perhaps, but it would do for transportation. He rode it to the rack in front of Paco's, then went inside.

It wasn't quite as dark as the hole at Rimshaw Prison but almost—or so it seemed after bright sunlight. An odor of old cigars and beer reached him. It took a few moments for his eyes to adjust.

Three men who had been drinking at the bar left as Lassiter entered. There were no other customers—just a long-haired girl who was talking to a big-armed barkeep. He knew instantly who she was. She looked around at Lassiter standing just inside the door, with no sign of recognition, which was understandable because she had seen him from a distance, as he had seen her. His eyes had evidently been sharper than hers. Even in the dim light he could see a hardness around her mouth as she watched him come to the bar.

He ordered a beer which the big barkeep set out. Then the man went back to talking to the girl at the end of the bar. Finally she said, "See you tonight, Barney," and started for the door.

Lassiter reached out and hooked her arm, which brought her to a sudden halt. She came thumping down on the high heels of her black slippers.

As she started to get angry, he said, "I heard Lassiter's out."

"Lassiter?" She looked at him blankly and made ineffectual passes at his strong fingers that gripped her arm.

"Timmie Borling's partner," Lassiter reminded.

"Oh, *him*." Then she frowned. She was rather pretty in an earthy way. "How can Lassiter be out? He's got years to serve."

"Where'd you get the money to give Borling?"

The abrupt question caused her to lose color and her eyes suddenly widened. "*You're* Lassiter!"

"Answer my question. Who paid you?"

She now clawed frantically at his hand. "Turn me loose," she hissed. And when his grip tightened, she squealed, "*Barney!*"

The big man charged around the end of the bar. And straight into Lassiter's hard right to the jaw. Eyes slightly crossed, Barney's knees caved. As he collapsed, his weight smashed one of the tables.

Lassiter put his attention back on the girl. "My hunch is it was somebody from Hopeville up north of here."

Felicia had been staring at Barney crumpled on the floor in the wreckage of the table. A man whistling, hands in pockets, started to enter the place. But he took one look, saw what was happening and quickly backed out and disappeared.

"You hit Barney an awful wallop," the girl said shakily.

"I didn't know if I still had it in me after all those months on the hill." He shook her. "Well, I'm waiting."

At last fear overcame a reluctance to talk. She said that a stranger had made her the proposition, a thousand dollars for her, a thousand for Joplin. She was to hide Joplin's money under a certain stone at the edge of the prison cotton patch where Borling would find it.

"Why such a roundabout way?" Lassiter wanted to know.

"He wanted you an' Borling, especially him, to think you were gonna escape for sure. You'd be on your way, then be cut down."

"As Timmie Borling was."

"So I heard." She looked up into his tight face. "Honest, that's all I know, Lassiter."

Lassiter asked her to describe the stranger. All she remembered was that he was quite handsome, heavily built, over six feet tall and well dressed. "An' he had a full beard."

"What name did he give you?"

"He never said."

"Why didn't you just take the money and clear out?"

" 'Cause I was scared of him an' he knew it. I figured he'd kill me if I tried to double-cross. So I never asked questions."

"Tell me more about him," Lassiter urged, letting her go. She stood rubbing the arm he had been gripping.

"The fella seemed to think it was all kind of a big joke. He laughed a lot. Soft-like laughter."

She glanced at Barney, who was emitting snorting

sounds and beginning to stir. Then she turned to Lassiter. "Take me with you wherever you figure to go," she whispered. "I'm sick of this place."

"I'm not forgetting that you had a hand in Timmie Borling getting killed," Lassiter reminded her coldly.

"Honest, Lassiter, I was scared not to do what the stranger wanted. You got any idea who he is?"

"Maybe." He was thinking of Borling's widow, Delira, and the man she was rumored to have taken up with. She intended to marry him, Timmie Borling had heard the rumor, as soon as the divorce went through. But he had never learned his name.

Lassiter left the girl, who by then was trying to help Barney up from the wrecked table.

He rode north. The only clue he had was a meager description of a handsome bearded man. A man who laughed a lot, she had said, soft-like laughter.

It had been a hard ride across the territory and Lassiter was glad to see the Crossroads ahead. It was a way station of sorts, a two-story building with a barn, sheds and a large corral. Today there were only three horses in the corral, none at the hitching post in front of the place.

He slid from the back of the weary roan and tied it to the post. He stretched his legs, looking around. Across the road grew clumps of oak and pine. Ruts in the two roads that crossed in front of the place were worn deep. No sound came from the building.

The sun, by now having lost most of its heat, had swung far to the west where it would soon poise like a huge ball before falling into the abyss of night. Lassiter's own shadow on the dusty ground was long as he climbed a few steps and entered the building. A bell above the door tinkled. This signaled a plump, unshaven man sitting on a stool behind the bar. He stood up and leaned his plump arms on the bar.

Lassiter started to speak, remembering him as Lew Oliver, the owner. But Oliver spoke first. "What can I do for you, *stranger?*" he asked through stiffened lips. His ghastly smile was obviously forced.

It produced a tingle at Lassiter's nape—always a warning of trouble. A quick look around showed only two tables, chairs, a counter and some shelves. But there seemed to be no one else.

"I'll take a beer," Lassiter said, putting his attention back on the nervous fat man behind the bar. Oliver extracted a bottle from a cooler and set it on the bar. With his left hand Lassiter uncorked it. His right hand hung free, inches from the holstered .44 at his belt.

The beer was lukewarm but satisfying. He had taken no more than two swallows when he was alerted by a soft scrape of boot leather against the floor. Turning carefully in the direction of the sound, he saw a large man with bushy eyebrows emerge from the kitchen. One cheek bulged with a chaw of tobacco. A gun jiggled at his belt as he came toward the bar. His pants were greasy canvas and his flannel shirt was badly faded.

"You come far?" he drawled, leaning against the end of the bar.

"Far enough."

"You're Lassiter, ain't you?"

Lassiter countered with, "Who're you?" He wasn't

about to give anything away to a stranger. Lew Oliver behind the bar was shifting from one foot to the other, his face slick with perspiration.

The big stranger said, "You're Lassiter, all right. You was described to me an' you're comin' from the right direction."

"Meaning where?"

"Rimshaw Prison."

Lassiter edged away from the bar. "What do you want?"

"You're to stay away from Hopeville. Step outside an' I'll tell you why."

"What if I don't want to stay away?"

The man's smile was ugly. "You figure it out." Without taking his eyes from Lassiter, he spat tobacco juice into a cuspidor. His aim was poor. Some of it stained the floor.

"Get your butt in the saddle and clear out!" Lassiter's voice crackled in the strained silence.

"Hey, Petey!" Rupe Sagar yelled. "Time to climb Lassiter's back!"

A door banged open across the long room. At the same moment Lassiter vaulted the bar, one hand on the top, the other gripping his .44. Rupe Sagar was drawing his gun but when Lassiter fired a bullet into his right shoulder, the gun clattered to the floor.

As Lassiter came down on both feet behind the bar, a gun from the doorway was fired. A bullet banged off a metal brewery sign behind the bar and shot out a corner of a window. The nervous Oliver was face down on the floor, trembling.

Before Petey, in a faded red shirt, could get set

again, Lassiter fired. Petey Sagar reeled backwards, losing his balance and plunging into the road.

At the end of the bar on the floor, a moaning Rupe Sagar clawed under his shirt with the left hand. Intricate metal work sparkled in the setting sun as he laboriously pointed the weapon. An instant before the weapon was fired, Lassiter twisted aside. As a bullet drilled a hole in the wall, Lassiter's .44 fired again. Rupe Sagar dropped his second gun to the floor and collapsed across both weapons.

Mindful of Petey, who he had last seen in the doorway, Lassiter backed to where Rupe Sagar was stretched out.

Lew Oliver was peering over the top of his bar at the man on the floor. "He dead?" he asked nervously.

"Might be," Lassiter said, bending over the man. He felt angry at himself for walking into this trap. Had his wits not been sharp it could have ended tragically for him. "Any more of 'em around?" he demanded of Oliver.

"Only them two." He squinted at Lassiter. "You're almighty fast on the trigger, Lassiter."

"It pays to be sometimes." He leaned over Rupe Sagar, who was suddenly gasping for breath. His chest heaved and there was a blot of redness at his lips. "Who sent you, Sagar?"

"Go . . . to . . . hell."

"Tell me, dammit!"

"Petey . . . get this son of a bitch . . ." It was the last thing he said. His mouth hung open and his eyes rolled back in his head. A death rattle could be heard in the silence.

Gripping his gun, Lassiter crept to the doorway and

peered out. There was no sign of Petey. But there was a bloodied spot in the road where he had fallen. Ducking low, Lassiter trailed splotches of blood in the dust that led toward the barn. Already the sun was dipping below the horizon. The shadows were long. In the haze of twilight everything became indistinct.

Circling the barn, he entered on the far side. But there was no sign of the man he sought. In the big barn with its odors of hay and dust, he found a saddled horse. And next to it was more blood on the straw-littered floor and sign, indicating that a second horse had been tied there. Petey had evidently mounted, walked the horse out of the barn, then rammed in the spurs once he was clear of the Crossroads. Lassiter scanned the darkening horizon but could find no trace of the man.

And was there any sense in trying to run him down in the growing darkness? he asked himself.

Returning to the barn, he lit a match and looked at the brand on the saddled horse. It was Muleshoe, the brand of the late Timmie Borling. Was Delira the one who had a hand in trying to prevent his return to Hopeville? Or was it someone else on the ranch?

After unsaddling the horse and caring for his roan, he returned to the way station. Oliver had dragged Rupe Sagar out the rear door where he lay crumpled in the yard. Lassiter went through Sagar's pockets but found nothing that would indicate who had sent him.

"They've been hangin' around here, waitin' to see if you'd come this way," Oliver said with a shake of the head. "I tried to warn you by callin' you 'stranger.' "

"I know and thanks."

Oliver's wife cooked him supper and he paid for a room.

Upstairs, he wedged a chair under the doorknob and slept with his gun on the floor beside his bed. Lying in the darkness, he thought about the Sagars, who had been sent by somebody at Muleshoe. Either Borling's widow or the man she planned to marry was the only way Lassiter could figure it. His main concern, however, was Borling's son Rance. It was the least he could do in Timmie Borling's memory. . . .

# Chapter Five

Delira Borling came out of her bath, her flesh rosy from the hot scented water. Flinging on a wrapper that soon showed dark patches from the moisture on her body, she sat down on a needlepoint chair and started brushing her long dark red hair. She had a classical face, a high forehead, pale brows above light gray eyes. Her lips were full and red. Her delicate chin could be firm on occasion whenever something displeased her. She was twenty-three and had been married to Timmie Borling for nearly two years.

Tonight was the school dance and she'd had Senna, the cook, prepare a delicious cold supper that she would take in a box wrapped in tissue paper. Craig Moran would offer the highest bid, of course, so they could eat together without gossip.

Trying to be discreet until the divorce came through had been a trial. Then Timmie had miraculously solved the problem by getting himself killed while trying to escape from prison. Probably it was just as well because the divorce proceedings had dragged on and on without a judgment being rendered. With only a divorce it wouldn't have been so easy for her to gain control over Muleshoe Ranch, which Timmie Borling had inherited from his first wife, so she had been told. But as his widow she had it all. Of course, there was one minor irritation—Timmie's young son Rance.

Since she had received the news of the death of her husband, Craig Moran had tried to pressure Delira into marrying him. But she kept putting him off, loving the feel of power she had. Her father used to say that she was as stubborn as a mule sometimes. The way she kept avoiding the subject of marriage whenever Craig brought it up, she supposed, was a perfect example of what her father had been talking about.

During the last argument on the subject, she had declared, "But, Craig darling, I'm a *widow*. I'm supposed to wait a year before remarrying."

"Nonsense," Moran had stormed. Her attitude infuriated him. However, she knew better than to push him too far, aware of his violent temper. He was usually dabbling in nefarious schemes of one kind or another that had nothing to do with his job as foreman of Muleshoe. She had even found the false beard recently among his things. When asked about it he laughed softly and took it from her, saying he'd been playing a joke on somebody. It was at a time when he had been gone from the ranch for a little less than a month. He was an experienced cattleman, which she soon recognized. When Timmie had been sent to prison she knew it was imperative to get someone capable to run the ranch for her. Moran, who happened to be passing through Hopeville, made himself available.

She gave herself a critical inspection in a mirror, then pinned up her hair. Finally, she dropped a polka-dot cotton frock over her head, then called on dumpy, flat-footed Senna to help with the buttons. Senna was a widow whose late husband had been a Muleshoe cowhand, finally raised to *segundo*.

Delira donned a light wrap and went downstairs to wait for Senna to bring up the buggy. As she stood at a window, admiring the peaceful twilight scene of fading light through tall trees, of pinpricks of stars beginning to unfold in the sky, she realized she had a visitor. A visitor unexpected and unwanted. Her face clouded when through the window she saw the boy on the veranda just about to knock. At first, upon hearing furtive footsteps on the porch, she thought it might be Craig coming to sneak a kiss before the school dance. She found herself getting deliciously excited just thinking about it.

Delira flung open the door and confronted the startled boy.

"Can I come in?" the boy asked solemnly. There was hint of an early moon in the purple sky.

"What are you doing here, Rance?" she asked crossly.

"I ran away."

"You had no right to leave the Adderlys."

"He . . . he got drunk and he whipped me." Rance pulled up a pant leg to show her the raw places on his leg. The sight of them made her cringe, but she wouldn't give in.

"Probably you deserved it," she snapped.

"You wouldn't talk that way if Poppa were here."

"Well, your Poppa isn't here and never will be again."

At mention of his dead father, the boy's chin trembled. "Can I go upstairs to my room?"

"I'd rather you didn't, Rance."

"But why not?" The boy was agitated, apparently close to tears.

"When your father went away, he left you in my care. And I was to use my own judgment in raising you."

"But my father's dead. . . ."

"And I'm his widow, Rance. So I still must do what I think is best for you. Best for us all. And that is for you to live with the Adderlys. At least for the present."

"I hate it there!"

"Part of growing up is learning to adjust to life. And you must learn to adjust to those people."

"I don't want to go back."

"By the way, how did you get out here?"

"I . . . I found a pony."

"Perhaps stole one." Delira shook her head. "You can get yourself in deep trouble doing things like that. And bring disgrace on the family name." Getting a firm grip on his small shoulder, she walked him out to the veranda and shouted into the twilight, "I need some help here!"

Two men came at a run. One was the giant Joplin, the other a lank rider named Ellick, whom Joplin waved aside. He came on alone, climbed the veranda steps and politely removed his hat from a mass of lank brown hair.

Delira always felt uneasy around the man and wished Craig hadn't hired him. When asked about the man, Craig Moran made an offhand remark about Joplin once having had something to do with Rimshaw Prison, which meant he must have had some connection with her late husband. Just what, she didn't know. And she didn't want to know, she told herself.

"Take the boy back to town, if you will, Joplin," she said, trying to be her regal best in the face of the leer that always seemed to lurk in his yellowish eyes.

"Yes, ma'am," he said and pinned the boy's two wrists in one meaty hand. "Where do I take him?"

"The Adderly house. He lives there. They're probably worried sick about him running away like this. He can show you the house. But if he won't, anyone can tell you where it is."

She listened to the sounds made by Rance's small boots as he was dragged across the veranda and down the steps.

Delira stepped back into the house and closed the door. Senna appeared from her quarters at the rear of the house. "Did I hear somebody, Mrs. Borling?"

Delira told her that Rance had run away again. Senna smoothed her brown dress over ample hips but made no comment.

Somehow the evening was spoiled for Delira.

Senna drove the buggy in silence to Hopeville. A sickle moon hung above the trees that bordered the schoolyard and the sky was filled with a trillion glittering diamonds.

Inside the sprawling building, Delira gave stiff smiles

to those who came up to speak to her. The ones who knew her well kept their distance, for they could read the fury in her gray eyes; something or someone this evening had displeased her, they knew.

Even during the spirited bidding for the box suppers, she had no interest. Funds raised this night were to go to the purchase of a new school bell.

As the bidding progressed, each winner received a round of applause. The beaming couple, usually hand in hand, went to tables set up in one of the school rooms. Perversely, Delira almost wished Craig would lose out in the bidding. He was up against a cowboy from the Box-S outfit who seemed bent on outbidding Craig and kept batting his eyes at Delira. He was rather loathsome, she decided, and wanted Craig to win after all.

Craig finally did win. "You seem in a sour mood tonight," he commented under his breath as they found room at one of the long tables. She decided to blame it on the boy, although there were many factors involved in producing her mood. She had wanted Craig with a feverish passion and now that she had him she found him to sometimes border on the monotonous. Why couldn't someone exciting enter her life?

She composed herself, and while daintily nibbling fried chicken, told Craig about Rance running way.

"What he needs is a good strapping," Moran said roughly.

"Indeed he does." She tested the roast; it was overdone. Her eyes darted wickedly about the dancing couples in the adjoining room, settling on Senna, who was in the arms of the town's strutting postmaster. "Senna made a mess of the roast."

"Why don't you ship the kid away?" Craig Moran said, returning to the subject of Rance Borling. "The way I see it, you don't owe him a damn thing."

"We'll think about it." She saw Jim Sloan edge his tall, lank figure through the crowd around the doorway, beaming at friends, grasping hands of menfolk, embracing ladies when he thought it proper. Right after receiving news of Timmie's death, he had called at the ranch, saying, "There'll be a line a mile long of young bloods askin' for your hand. I ain't so much a young blood but I'm almighty in love with you. Have been ever since you came here."

She had put him off politely, having no desire to be known in Crissman County as wife of a sheriff. She planned on reaching higher stations in life.

He saw her now sitting with Craig Moran, but didn't come over. He gave them a wave of the hand instead, looking a little enviously at Craig, she thought.

Craig was back on the subject of the boy. "I'd prefer him out from under when we're married, Delira. A military school oughta be fine for him." He reached out and clasped her hand. "And speaking of marriage, we could have the Reverend Lynde perform the ceremony at any time. How about tomorrow?"

She squirmed in her chair. "That would be rushing things and you know it," she said crossly. "I need time. . . ." Her voice trailed away and she became utterly still, her mouth hanging open.

"What's the matter?" Craig hissed above the sound of voices and the music from the next room.

"Over there . . . by the door. Lassiter."

Craig jerked around in his chair to peer over his shoulder. He had been chewing but now his jaws ceased their motion. "I'll be damned," he breathed. "What a nerve that bastard's got."

Delira placed her hand over her heart, feeling it swell and pound. Her breathing became shallow and she sagged limply back in her chair as she stared at the tall, dark figure.

"Your face is flushed," she heard Craig saying.

"I . . . I had a feeling all along that we hadn't seen the last of Lassiter," she managed to say.

"He won't hurt you," he snapped.

Hurt me, Craig? she wanted to say. What is the opposite of hurt? It is pleasure, which is now firing my brain. . . .

Moran was rigid as he stared at Lassiter, realizing the Sagar brothers had failed him.

# Chapter Six

Lassiter saw her through the crowd, sitting slim and elegant at a table with a rather handsome man. Attired in new work clothes purchased with some of the funds allotted him by the territory, Lassiter threaded his way toward their table.

"Lassiter," Delira bubbled, wearing her best smile. "I honestly didn't expect to see you again."

The handsome man stood up. He was taller than Lassiter. His expensively tailored dark suit subtly revealed an imposing physique.

"I'd like you to meet Craig Moran," Delira said. "Craig, this is Lassiter. I'm sorry I only know you by the one name. . . ."

"Lassiter's good enough." He eyed Moran coldly, feeling he was the one Delira had acquired when her husband had been sent to prison. Now she was in line for better things—another marriage. Neither man extended a hand at the introduction but stood staring at each other. Delira kept licking her lips nervously. Others nearby, aware of the tension, were suddenly silent.

"Where is the boy?" Lassiter asked, looking around.

"What business is it of yours?" Moran asked sharply.

"I owe it to Timmie Borling to see that his son's all right," Lassiter replied.

"I assure you, he is quite all right," Delira said hastily.

"Now you may leave," Moran said, nodding toward the door.

"I want to see Rance," Lassiter said softly. Around him swirled aromas of the various boxed suppers open on the tables, mixed with cigar smoke and perfume. Everyone was staring.

"After you see him, then what?" Delira asked, searching his face.

"I figure to see that he gets what is due him as Timmie Borling's son."

"I resent your implication that he might not get what is due him," Delira snapped, her good mood suddenly gone. She started to say more but Craig Moran interrupted with a lifted hand.

"It won't hurt to let him see the kid," Moran said smoothly and Delira looked up at him with a frown. Moran smiled. "Come, I'll show you where he is."

Moran started for the door, skirting Lassiter. Suddenly, he spun around and swung his fist at Lassiter's face. But Lassiter was prepared for treachery. As the blow came whistling toward his face, Lassiter tilted his head. And the fist slid across the top of his shoulder instead of catching him in the face.

With a roar of anger, Moran attacked him and the

two men grappled and swayed and bumped into a table. Dishes crashed to the floor. A woman with a lapful of gravy began to scream.

Then the two men were wrestling each other across the dance floor, with couples trying to get out of their way. As hammering blows were exchanged, the piano, fiddle and cornet gradually faded into discord, then silence.

Men were shouting. "They'll wreck the place!"

Locked together, Lassiter worked his arm free but Moran nearly succeeded in kneeing him. Lassiter slammed him on the right cheekbone, splitting the skin. Blood gushed down Moran's face.

Finally, bystanders seized the two men, keeping them apart. As they milled around the doorway, Sheriff Jim Sloan came strutting up, his thumbs hooked in the armholes of his vest.

"What's goin' on here?" he demanded quietly, his eyes sliding from one combatant to the other.

Moran had been allowed to use a handkerchief on his bleeding face. His hazel eyes were venomous. "Lassiter cursed me under his breath, something I won't stand for!"

"You are a damned liar," Lassiter said through his teeth, which brought a gasp from onlookers.

Sheriff Sloan fixed a pale eye on Lassiter. "I can appreciate what you've been through. But it don't give you the right to come up here an' raise holy hell . . . beggin' your pardon, ladies," he added, looking around at the many strained female faces.

"Outside we go!" Craig Moran whipped a fist into

the air above his head, teeth bared. It brought a shout. "You ready, Lassiter?"

A crowd of exuberant men surged around Lassiter and literally shoved him out into the schoolyard. A few clouds had rolled in, blanking out the moon and dimming the stars. Lassiter scowled. What he didn't need now was a senseless brawl. And yet he was committed to it. He couldn't back out now.

A few males lingered inside the schoolhouse, probably to satisfy admonitions of their wives not to encourage trouble by witnessing it.

Lassiter had taken only a couple of steps, when he felt a hand on his arm. Looking around, he saw Delira's pale face.

"Don't do it, Lassiter," she said huskily. "Craig has fought all over the West. . . ."

"So have I. In one form or another."

"But he's been a champion in Nevada. This I know for sure."

"Makes no difference . . ."

"A man came through a few weeks ago and recognized him. He spread the word."

"The food will go to waste," a woman wailed.

"I want to see you, Lassiter . . . alone," Delira said above the babble of voices. "Meet me tomorrow. Noon. At the top of Pride's Point. You know where it is."

He looked at her and nodded. Across the yard Sheriff Sloan was arguing with Moran. "But I don't want trouble, Moran," the sheriff was saying.

"It's a night for trouble," said Moran with a laugh. He had removed his coat, which he handed to one of his sycophants. Then he began rolling his shirtsleeves over powerful forearms.

"I'm askin' you not to do this, Moran," the sheriff persisted, but Moran ignored him.

But several angry men added their own voices, pointing out to Moran that a lot of preparation had gone into this night, and it shouldn't be spoiled by a brawl.

As Lassiter edged closer through the crowd of on-lookers, he heard more heated protests, and at last Moran said, "All right, boys. I'll back off. For now."

Sheriff Sloan had already spotted Lassiter over his shoulder and now spun around. "No you don't, Lassiter. I'm here to keep the peace. I've talked Moran into staying away from you," he said sternly, taking all the credit for Moran's decision. "You clear out—you don't belong here."

A smile touched Lassiter's lips. "If you say so, Sheriff."

"I do say so. And as long as you're going, it might be a good idea for you to get out of town. Clear out of the valley."

"Quit leaning on me, Sheriff," Lassiter said, a hard edge to his voice now, no longer faintly amused by the sheriff's attitude. He could see Moran looking at him as he put on his coat. There was a smug expression on the man's face.

"Let's have some music!" the sheriff called, and the piano player ran a few chords, which drew the fiddler and then the cornetist. People began to dance again.

Lassiter walked down to the Trail's End for a drink,

thinking about this meeting at noon tomorrow with Delira. Ceiling lamps behind copper shades sizzled and smoked. There were only a few customers. Nearly everyone, it seemed, was attending the school dance. Music from the direction of the school could be faintly heard above the buzz of talk.

He was halfway through his "sippin' whiskey" when a boy wearing a cap, a lock of reddish hair sticking out, came bounding in on long legs. He looked around. "Which one's Lassiter?"

"I am," Lassiter said, and the boy came over while the other customers looked on curiously.

"Lady wants to see you outside," the boy said, panting.

"Tell her to come in here if she wants to see me so bad."

The boy looked horrified. "A lady can't come in *here!*"

And Lassiter had to admit that he was right; ladies didn't enter saloons, especially those of the caliber of the Trail's End. Providing she was a lady, that is.

Assuming it was Delira who wanted to see him, he finished his drink. Before Lassiter and Timmie Borling had gotten into trouble, she had been sending suggestive signals when her husband wasn't around. Provocative looks, an exaggerated swing of hips when she walked away, a touch of warm fingers on the back of his hand when she leaned close to tell him something. It annoyed and embarrassed Lassiter; after all, Timmie was his friend. He had been about to tell Timmie Borling he was moving along when Dave Ashburn had been murdered and they were arrested.

He followed the boy who was holding open one of

the swinging doors. He stepped out into the darkness and the boy scampered away. Instantly, Lassiter was alert and dropped a hand to his gun on the chance he had been lured into an ambush.

But a voice harsh with scorn cut at him from the shadows. A woman's voice. "You were pointed out to me, Mr. Lassiter, in case you're wondering how I knew you."

A tall girl stepped into view where a cone of light spilled from saloon windows. Her hair was so dark it seemed to make her light blue eyes vivid. Her lips were full, the chin firm and uptilted. She wore a shirt and a vest and divided riding skirt.

"Who're you?" be demanded softly.

"Ellen Stencoe."

"Stencoe?" Lassiter asked in surprise.

"I see the name means something to you."

"His confession is one of the reasons I'm here, Miss Stencoe."

"My brother never killed that man Ashburn."

"Your brother?"

"Yes, my brother." Her voice broke. "He was much older than I. And always very good to me. I . . . I intend to find out who murdered him and see them brought to justice."

Lassiter was eyeing her. "Your brother wasn't murdered. He shot himself."

She gave such a violent shake of her head that a thick braid came tumbling down from her head. She brushed it impatiently aside and leaned forward, her eyes bright with anger. "Who did you pay, Mr. Lassiter, to write out a fake confession and then kill my brother?"

That surprised him. "Listen . . ." He stepped closer, but she backed quickly away. She came up against a wall of the Trail's End.

"I'm warning you, Lassiter. I intend to get to the bottom of this foul mess. If I have to stay in this awful place a year or more!"

"Will you give me a chance to talk?" Her attitude was beginning to exasperate him.

"Go ahead, talk."

"The confession came as a bigger surprise to me than to anyone else."

"That I doubt. . . ." Her lips twisted in scorn.

"Believe me on that, Miss Stencoe. And as for me hiring anyone to kill your brother, it's not true." He had softened his voice and at the last she blinked at him and looked away.

"It . . . it's what I was told. That you were behind it."

"Who told you?" He caught her by a wrist, his fingers pressing harder than intended.

"A man named . . . you're hurting me." And when he dropped her wrist, she rubbed it and said, "A man named Moran. Craig Moran."

A bomb went off in Lassiter's skull. Seizing her by the hand, he literally dragged her along the walk while she desperately tried to keep up with his long-legged stride without stumbling.

"Where . . . where are we going?" she finally managed to gasp.

"To the school dance," he snapped, his beak of a nose cutting through the dry night air.

"But I'm not dressed for a dance," she panted.

"I don't intend to dance with you, Miss Stencoe."

"Then what in the world . . . ?"

By then they had reached the schoolyard. In the light of numerous lanterns there was a gasp as those in the yard saw who had returned.

A bearded man spoke up. "Moran's gone, if you're lookin' for him."

Lassiter halted his mad plunge across the schoolyard, Ellen Stencoe coming to a stumbling halt in his wake. He released her moist hand.

"Where'd he go?" Lassiter demanded of the bearded man.

"They had a spat, him an' Mrs. Borling. Went home, I reckon."

"Home likely bein' her place," said a plump woman with a nasty voice.

Ellen Stencoe was flexing the fingers of the hand that Lassiter had grasped. "You're a madman, Lassiter," she gasped. "Lord knows what trouble you'd have gotten us into."

Someone had told Sheriff Sloan about Lassiter's return, which brought him hurrying out of the schoolhouse, wiping his lips on a napkin tucked into his shirtfront. He was chewing.

"I thought I told you . . ." He shook a long forefinger under Lassiter's nose.

"I wanted to see Moran. To make him correct some things he told this young lady."

Sloan looked at Ellen Stencoe, then said gruffly, "I know her. She introduced herself the day she struck town."

"You practically ridiculed me," she began, her voice shaking.

"I told her right off that there was no sense to what she claimed about her brother. You oughta be thankful, Lassiter, that he up an' confessed. Otherwise you wouldn't be standin' here."

Lassiter turned to speak to the girl, but she had slipped away in the darkness. He didn't feel like going after her. Another day he could try and reason with her.

"It's a good thing Moran wasn't here," Sloan was saying. "You made a move against him an' I'd have had to lock you up."

"Maybe a good thing, maybe not."

"You don't take advice worth a damn, do you, Lassiter?" The sheriff jerked the napkin from his shirt and stuffed it into a pocket. "I told you it was best if you left here. But you didn't listen. . . ."

With a snort of disgust, Lassiter turned his back and walked away. He thought perhaps the sheriff would call him back or come after him, but he didn't.

Sleep that night in his hotel room was hard to come by. To learn that Bert Stencoe had an avenging relative, an attractive young lady at that, had been upsetting. Lying on his back, fingers laced behind his head, he stared up at the water-marked ceiling and pondered her theory that her late brother had not murdered Ashburn, written a confession then killed himself.

How close it came to what Lassiter himself had been thinking over since Superintendent Galendor had given him his freedom down at Rimshaw Prison.

Then he found Delira creeping into his consciousness with her sulky manner, giving him sidelong glances out of her gray eyes. He was remembering her suggestion of a meeting at Pride's Point. Come morning, he'd think about meeting her at noon.

He listened to the creaking of the hotel, men laughing as they came out of the Trail's End. Their boots made scuffing sounds on the plank walk. He heard muffled hoofbeats, then finally silence, save for the distant yelping of coyotes.

So far he had not seen Rance Borling, the main object of his return to Hopeville. Tomorrow he would find the boy and have a long talk. It seemed only months ago instead of years when Lassiter had stopped by Muleshoe to see Timmie Borling. After some years of knocking around, Borling had in effect hit the jackpot with his marriage, where he acquired not only Rancine as a bride but a vast holding known as Muleshoe Ranch. But the ranch had been suffering since the death of Rancine's father and it had taken hard work on Borling's part to put it back on its feet.

Lassiter was instantly drawn to Rancine, a radiant beauty. The last time he saw her she was with child and quite happy about it, as was Borling. Lassiter was in El Paso when a letter from Borling caught up with him. Rancine had died giving birth to their son. Lassiter went north to console his old friend, then pushed on. It was later that Borling asked him to help out at Muleshoe. Although Borling acted as his own foreman, he needed a *segundo* he could trust. He wanted Lassiter to fill that role. While mourning for his dead wife, Borling explained, he had let things go to hell.

This time Lassiter stayed for a few months, then drifted again. The next time he heard from Timmie

Borling was to announce a wedding. Although Lassiter didn't make it for the wedding, he did show up some months later. Delira was as pretty as Rancine, but in a different way—brittle, more superficial.

The first time they were alone, Delira looked at him slyly and said, "You're the first of Timmie's friends that promises some excitement around here."

There were other incidents which caused Lassiter to stay away from her as much as possible.

One day Borling seemed upset. "I got a feelin' you don't like Delira," he complained.

"Sure I do." Lassiter forced a smile.

He had again taken over the job of *segundo,* but wanted to get away. He was beginning to think up excuses for moving on when their partner at the weekly poker games was found shot in the back. A half-dozen gunshots had shattered his spine.

Was Delira up to her old tricks, wanting him to meet her tomorrow? But as he turned it over in his mind he thought he owed it to the memory of Timmie Borling to find out what she wanted.

In the early morning he made small talk with Silas Rimmley, the bewhiskered, raw-boned owner of the store, who was dusting his shelves. He peered at Lassiter through wire-framed spectacles, remembering him from his sporadic associations with the late Timmie Borling. His look was of disapproval as if still believing him guilty of Dave Ashburn's murder, despite the written confession of Bert Stencoe.

"Why do you want to know where the boy is, anyhow, Lassiter?" Rimmley growled.

"I owe it to Borling to see that his son is making out all right."

Rimmley frowned, continued with his dusting for a few moments, then looked carefully around. There was no one else in the store. He lowered his voice. "Tell you the truth, I never cared much for Borling's second wife. Now the first one, she was a lady. . . ."

"I'm only interested in the boy, Rimmley."

"Was gettin' to that. The kid don't seem happy to me."

"How do you mean?"

"He was always a bright little fellow when his pa was around. But now it's like he's livin' deep in a cave. Hard to get anything out of him."

Lassiter tried to be casual. "Where is he?"

"Mrs. Borling farmed him out with the Adderlys." Rimmley made a face and told Lassiter where he could find the house. Lassiter thanked him and started for the door. "Maybe it's only my imagination, me thinkin' the boy ain't happy," the store owner called after him, as if deciding at the last minute to play it safe and not risk antagonizing Delira Borling.

Maude Adderly proved to be a heavyset, suspicious woman who peered at him from a front window. Although Lassiter had knocked on the door, she hadn't opened it.

"I'd like to see Rance Borling," he explained through the window.

"Who're you?"

When Lassiter told her she sniffed. "I heard of you." She looked him over, then said, "You can see the boy for a minute, as long as you're so set on it."

"I'd like to see him alone."

"Ain't possible."

It was so shadowed inside the house that Lassiter had only a vague impression of the woman's plump face and her bulky figure. She kept back from the window as if afraid he might reach in and seize her.

"Wait right where you're at, Lassiter," she said, and marched into another part of the house.

After a few moments, Lassiter was aware of a whispered exchange between the woman and someone else. He cocked his head, trying to listen, but could make nothing out.

"Rance, there's a fella wants to see you," the woman suddenly bellowed.

"Yes . . . ma'am," came a small voice.

Presently, there was a thump of small boots as Rance Borling appeared and came up to the window where he stared out at Lassiter on the porch.

"'Lo, Lassiter. What . . . what do you want, anyhow?"

"I want to see you." Lassiter saw the boy swallow and lick his lips nervously. "How've you been, Rance?"

The woman, who stood in deep shadows, her heavy arms folded across her chest, hissed something at the boy.

"Lassiter, you . . . you helped get my pa in trouble. . . ." the boy began in a thin, quavering voice.

"Look, I want to set you straight on a few things. . . ."

But the boy cut him off by turning his back and walking stiffly away.

"Rance!" Lassiter called to him.

"I don't want to talk to you none!" The boy glanced over his shoulder, but it was so dark Lassiter couldn't make out the expression on the small face. But he had an impression that it was fear.

Mrs. Adderly came to the window and gave Lassiter a vicious smile. "You satisfied?" she snarled, then banged down the window.

All along Lassiter had sensed the woman and possibly her husband had given the boy whispered instructions—in some way threatening him. Although angered at the possiblity, Lassiter decided to let it ride for the present.

After his meeting with the boy's stepmother, then he'd see. . . .

# Chapter Seven

Leaving town to the east, in case anyone was watching him, Lassiter eventually swung west. Soon he was in the midst of vast acres of sage that sloped up toward the gigantic red cliffs that hovered over the basin. After some miles, he crossed a level stretch and slipped through a narrow chasm in yellow walls of stone, an opening just wide enough for a horse and rider.

"A good place to remember," he recalled Timmie Borling telling him once, "in case you wants get away from somebody." This was followed by the familiar wink, a bark of laughter.

It was hard for Lassiter to realize that Borling was gone. He'd been just a cowhand really, who'd had a little education and drifted, as had Lassiter, until finding his luck shining so bright that it hurt the eyes, as Borling had put it when recounting the meeting with Rancine, his first wife. He had come to work for the "old man" as they called his late wife's father. He and Rancine took a liking to each other right off and it wasn't long before they were meeting surreptitiously at Pride's Point.

One day it had ended in near disaster when they were found by her suspicious father. In his rage, the old man threatened to kill Borling and drew a gun, which Timmie Borling took away from him, careful not to hurt the older man. Then Borling talked quickly and reasonably with Rancine clinging to his arm, backing up everything Timmie said.

"Dad, we want to get married. . . ."

"A helluva way to go about it," the old man had stormed. "Sneakin' out like a couple of . . ." He couldn't finish it.

For weeks Rancine had wanted to tell her father, but every time Timmie Borling suggested it was time for them to face him, she backed off, dreading her father's wrath.

Everyone of importance in the county attended the wedding celebration that lasted for three days.

Many times on long prison nights Timmie Borling recounted the sequence of events until Lassiter knew it by heart.

It was all running through his mind as he moved along the vent in the yellow walls, which ended at a towering spire. Piñon pines were clustered around its base, which was tangled with buckbrush. The easier ascent to the point, which could be made by horseback, was off the road, directly opposite from where he was sitting in his saddle. It took him only a few moments to settle it in his own mind. He chose the steeper, more dangerous route to the top of the point.

Seen from below at certain angles, the top seemed to be in the form of an arrow that pointed due west. An early settler, Tom Pride, had named it Arrow Point, but after he was killed by marauders, the name was changed to Pride's Point.

Leaving his horse, Lassiter started climbing a narrow trail through the brush, his long legs propelling him upward at a fast pace. But he was careful where he stepped, avoiding stones that could be dislodged or dry brush. He wanted no proof of his arrival until there was a chance to study the lay of the land. The point itself was a great circular stone, some fifty yards across at its base, used for centuries by Indians as a lookout. He glanced at the sun which was still in its ascendancy. Delira had said noon, but he was intentionally early. He breathed deeply of air scented with pine and creosote and the faint dust kicked up by his climb. A sheen of sweat covered his face and his shirt clung damply to his broad back. Upon being released from solitary confinement, he had been in a weakened condition but with the passing days his strength was returning rapidly. In fact, his breathing was only slightly labored when he reached the summit.

Once there, brush was a thick screen on all sides of a clearing some seventy feet across. There were numerous smoke-blackened rocks from old fires used by Indian scouts to keep warm or perhaps to send smoke signals.

Parting the brush, he looked south across the basin, seeing in the distance a haze of smoke that marked the site of Hopeville. As he drew back, he saw lying in the rocks a half-smoked slim cigar no more than a few days old. And a little farther on he found a dainty handkerchief edged in lace, wadded up and cast into the brush.

Somebody's keeping your bed warm, Timmie, Lassiter thought. It put a sad smile on his face. Or perhaps a cowboy and some girl from town or from one of the nearby ranches. A lonely existence for a girl. Rancine had hated it until Timmie Borling entered her life.

A tour of the area, peering at clumps of brush and into a maze of boulders big as sheds, produced no Delira. He wondered what she wanted to see him about and why she had picked such a lonely spot for their meeting. But as soon as it crossed his mind, he thought he had the answer. A grim smile touched his lips.

Determined to be on his guard, in case she had other plans, he checked his gun. Then he left it loose in the holster so there would be no bind of leather. He rolled a cigarette and lit it by thumbing a match alight. Drawing deeply on the cigarette he felt the hot smoke in his lungs.

The longer he waited, the more on edge he became because he began to wonder if he had foolishly stepped into a trap. Then his eyes squeezed into slits as he heard a sound. A hoof scraping stone? Here and there were clumps of grass and a few oaks that somehow had taken root to offer shade.

Stepping to the edge of the lookout, he studied the switchback horse trail below. He could see the town road clearly, but the only sign of movement was a freight outfit that from this distance seemed to be barely moving.

It reminded him of his own youth, when he had been driving a freight wagon for his father when he was eleven. They had never gotten along. He thought of the educated drifter with his satchel of books who signed on with his father. The books were loaned to Lassiter, who devoured them. Then, after breaking with his father, he'd finally drifted to Mexico where he, at his young age, became the right-hand man of a *hacendado* who wanted to learn English. By teaching him, Lassiter gained access to the rancher's vast library. But it had all ended during one of those senseless uprisings that periodically sweep Mexico.

Again he heard the sound—closer now—definitely the scrape of a hoof on rock. Drawing his gun, he waited. The steps he heard were light, possibly made by a pony. Presently, Delira, panting, came into view on a little mare. At first she didn't see him, then her gray eyes widened as she saw him holster his gun.

"Were you going to shoot me, Lassiter?" she asked with a strange little laugh.

"Are you alone?"

"Very much alone." She dismounted, tied her mare and sank to a wide flat rock. She fanned herself with her hat while watching him. She patted the stone slab where she was sitting. "There's room enough for you."

He didn't accept her offer but did rest one foot on the rock, leaning forward, crossed arms resting on his bent leg. "I want to talk about the boy. . . ."

"This is the spot where Timmie won himself a ranch and a bride," she interrupted. Tendrils of reddish hair clung to her damp brow. She wore a boy's shirt, the tails knotted in front so that it was snug across her breasts. "Do you have such aspirations, Lassiter?" she teased.

"I suppose Timmie told you this."

"Not in so many words. But I figured it out for myself. He told me once that Rancine's father caught them here . . . kissing, was the way he put it." She laughed softly. "Kissing."

Fawnskin riding pants were a second skin at her thighs and hip. Birds kept up a continuous chatter in the trees. Far below, his eyes caught a pinprick of movement. Adjusting his vision, he leaned forward to stare through the brush down at bobbing white tails of a herd of racing antelope, so distant he could barely make them out.

"Mainly I want to talk to you about the boy," he said, putting his attention back on her.

"Rance is in good hands."

"I don't think so."

"I understand you visited the Adderlys and were quite rude. That doesn't seem like you, Lassiter. You're much too charming to be rude." She was beaming up at him from the stone bench, lifting arms overhead as if to stretch away her weariness from the long climb. It made her breasts stir provocatively.

"Timmie thought the world of his son," Lassiter said. "It was the one thing he lived for."

Her mood changed suddenly. Her eyes darkened and a faint frown disturbed the smooth skin between them. "I'll raise the boy and do a good job. I can promise you that."

"I'm not so sure."

"As soon as . . . a certain situation has changed."

She was staring into the distance as if at hazy mountains barely visible to the south.

"What situation?" he asked.

"Craig Moran. You met him at the school dance."

"He seems to have you under his thumb."

She gave such a violent shake of her head that some of the dark red hair she'd fashioned atop her shapely head came tumbling down. "Never!" She groped for one of Lassiter's broad hands and held it in both of hers, explaining how Moran was constantly after her for marriage. How she was really afraid of him. "I . . . I'm even beginning to think he might have had something to do with Timmie's death."

Lassiter's face was a mask as he said, "Why do you say that?"

"Things he's said. Mostly at times when he's relaxed, let down, you might say. . . ."

"You mean after he's just had a woman." His smile was hard and for an instant her eyes sparked. Then she gave a little shrug.

"I'm not ashamed of anything I've ever done. Done invariably in a moment of weakness as with Craig. But I was so lonely after Timmie was sent to prison."

"You didn't show much loyalty to try and divorce him."

"That was one of my greatest moments of weakness, I admit." Her gray eyes were imploring as she gazed intently up into his face.

"It crushed Timmie when he heard about it."

"I . . . I can understand." Her two hands tightened on his.

70

"Tell me why you think Moran might have had something to do with Timmie's death," he asked softly.

"He took a trip just about that time, saying he had business with a cattle buyer. I didn't argue. I was glad to be rid of him for a while so I could try and think things through."

Lassiter's voice hardened. "A very handsome man, a certain girl working in a cantina described him. She was talking about the man who planned the fake escape. And Moran is . . . handsome, I admit."

"You have something against Craig already and that's good." She drew a deep breath, her abdomen expanding against the knotted shirttails, threatening to loosen them. "Lassiter, I'd like you to take back your old job."

*"Segundo?"*

"Foreman this time. I suppose superintendent for a ranch as big as Muleshoe is a better title." She leaned forward. "I'll be candid with you. The boy makes me nervous, having him underfoot. I'll send him away to a good school. You'll be here to see that I keep my promise."

"And what do I have to do?" he asked quietly, the beginnings of a sardonic smile forming on his lips. But she was looking across the valley and failed to notice.

"Fire Craig. Keep him away from me."

"With me as your husband, I suppose?" he drawled.

She appeared to ponder the possibility, then lifted her shoulders, and let them fall. The knot of shirttails at her waist was definitely loosening.

"Perhaps in time," she said seriously. "But for now I enjoy my freedom and sense of power."

71

"I see."

"Owning the ranch gives it to me, Lassiter." Her eyes blazed fiercely as she looked up at him again. "Do you understand?"

"Perfectly."

Something in his tone narrowed her eyes. "Did I detect sarcasm?" A sudden wisp of wind blew at her hair and tightened the front of her striped shirt. "I enjoy my power and I don't care who knows it."

"At least you come right to the point."

"But I am willing to share . . . with a strong man."

"Share with me, you mean? But not as a husband."

"Make Craig leave the country . . ."

"Or kill him."

". . . it's all I ask."

"Or kill him, I said," Lassiter repeated, which caused her cheeks to redden.

She set her small teeth and said, "Yes, if it comes to that."

He shook his head. "No thanks." Not for that reason, dear lady, he thought.

She released his hand. "But I thought you were ruthless. They say you are."

"I'm no murderer for hire."

She made a sound of exasperation. "I wasn't talking about murder," she said too loudly. "I only meant that if he got in the way and it came to guns that I . . . I wouldn't mourn his passing."

"Or mine, I suppose."

"What did you mean by that remark?"

"They hang murderers."

"They didn't hang you and Timmie," she reminded him archly.

"They might as well have, so far as Timmie's concerned. He's very dead."

"But you're very much alive." She took a deep breath, which drew his attention to her breasts. A small smile stirred the corners of her attractive mouth.

They were sitting together on the slab of rock, the wind in their faces. She was gesturing at the vast country below, saying that a great deal of it belonged to her. Lassiter corrected her, saying that by rights she had to share it with Timmie's son when he came of age. As he talked, she allowed her left hand to fall, as if by accident, across his lap. Then, moistening her lips, she leaned against him, her face upturned, a bold invitation in her eyes. But Lassiter didn't stir.

"Get the boy safe in that school we talked about and then . . ." He flashed a hard smile. "And then most anything can happen."

"I want it to happen now, this minute." She sounded cross; an imperial majesty being denied her pleasure.

A slight movement far below caught Lassiter's eye. Slipping off the stone slab, he crept to the edge of the lookout and peered down. Even from that height he recognized Craig Moran, who tied his horse in a cluster of pines away from the road then began to pace across the entrance to the lookout.

"What's he doing here?" Lassiter asked, keeping his voice low in case it might carry the hundred feet or so in the clear air.

Delira came to stand beside him, peering straight

down at the crown of Moran's hat and his heavy shoulders. "Oh, him." She gave an exaggerated shrug.

"Did you figure to get us here to shoot it out?"

"Never." She looked shocked.

"Best man wins or something like that?"

As he watched, six riders came at a gallop from the direction of Muleshoe, raising dust in the air.

Lassiter turned on her. "What kind of a trap did you set for me, anyhow?"

But this time she seemed genuinely bewildered. "Nobody else was supposed to be here . . . only Craig. . . ." As the admission slipped out, her face colored.

But Lassiter's attention was drawn to one particular rider who was approaching the spot where Moran waited stiffly. It gave Lassiter a start, for the man looked surprisingly like Meager Joplin. The same oversize build, dwarfing the horse he rode.

"What's Joplin doing here?" he hissed.

"He works for us. Craig hired him. He's from the prison. I suppose you know him."

"Oh, yeah, I know him." Lassiter's voice was hard.

"I dislike him intensely."

"You run the ranch, not Moran. Why don't you fire Joplin?"

And when she said nothing he knew then that Moran was truly in the saddle, not letting her have a say as to how Muleshoe was run. No wonder she wanted to get rid of him.

"Joplin's the one who killed your husband," Lassiter said roughly. "He killed Timmie."

"They'll go away in a minute or so and leave Craig here alone. . . ."

74

"Didn't you hear what I said? Joplin killed Timmie Borling!"

"I can't help that," she snapped.

"I realize all of a sudden that you didn't love Timmie at all. Probably never did!"

"Why, how dare you talk to me like that!"

She lunged, hands raised, fingers cupped like cat's claws. But he flung her aside when she tried desperately to rake his cheeks with her nails.

She fell to her knees and began screaming. "Craig! Help! Help!"

Down below, Craig Moran was glaring at Joplin. "What the hell are you doing here?"

Joplin reined in, flushing at the way Moran was yelling at him. "Right after you left the ranch, Petey Sagar come. He got a bullet slice across his thigh. Lassiter killed his brother Rupe. I figured you'd want to know, so I trailed you an' run into these boys an' they come along."

"Petey Sagar should've kept on going," Moran snarled.

And at that moment a woman's cry drifted down from above. It was someone screaming for help.

It took him a moment to realize it was Delira screaming. What the hell was she doing at the summit? And she had stressed that he was to meet her below, not above, that she was afraid to make the climb alone. Today he had intended having it out with her, forcing her into marriage.

The scream was repeated. Bounding into the saddle, he started for the switchbacks that would take him to the top. Behind him streamed the six men. The sounds of their horses being ridden recklessly boomed up the narrow trail.

Lassiter didn't wait but darted across the clearing and into the thick brush on the east side. Part of the steep, downward trail was grass-grown and slippery, but he kept his balance in the headlong flight. Staying to confront seven men was more odds than he cared to face. With his long legs pumping, one hand clamped to his gun to keep it from spilling from its holster, he ran. Near the bottom he leaped over a shallow wash and a thumb-sized stream of water. Today had proved something he had always suspected. Delira was pure bitch.

# Chapter Eight

A furious Delira saw Lassiter one moment and the next he was gone. She listened to his running footsteps, already beginning to fade. Angrily she caught her shirt in her two hands and ripped it. Buttons scattered in the sunlight.

Muleshoe men led by Craig Moran finally loomed up, bringing with them a fog of dust. Moran leaped from his mount that was lathered from the fast climb. The six other men drew rein, leaning over their saddlehorns to stare at the woman.

"Delira, what's happened?" Moran demanded, running to her.

She was hunched over, her teeth sunk in her lower lip, her hair wild about her face. Already she regretted her rash act of temper. With her two hands she held the front of the torn shirt over her breasts. But when Moran demanded to know who had been here to cause such a fright, she blurted Lassiter's name.

Moran drew his gun and yelled at his men. "Lassiter . . . get him!"

But a quick search of the brush showed no sign of him. However, Joplin discovered the foot trail and with three men went slipping and sliding downward.

Moran loomed over Delira. "What in hell are you doing up here, anyway?" he hissed.

"It's where I said I'd meet you."

"Hell you did. You told me to meet you below, right after noon."

"I wish you wouldn't use that word *hell*. It annoys me."

"You seem to have recovered pretty damn quick. What did Lassiter try to do to you?"

"Well, he didn't succeed. I . . . I fought him off."

He gave her a skeptical look, then boosted her into the saddle of her mare. He turned to the three remaining Muleshoe men. "When the others come back, take Lassiter's trail. When you catch up, hang him. He assaulted Mrs. Borling."

Delira and Moran rode in silence through clumps of piñons on their way back to the ranch headquarters. At one place in grassy plots, long petaled purple lilies were blooming.

Finally, Moran spoke. "What was your game today?"

"Game? To meet you. What else?"

"You said you were afraid to go to the top alone. That I should wait for you and we'd ride to the summit together."

"I wanted to overcome my fear and made the ride."

"What I meant by game was you pitting me against Lassiter."

She twisted in the saddle, her eyes blazing. "How incredibly stupid you are to even think such a thing!" But he only gave a smile that bit deeply and coldly to her very vitals. A shred of fear began to worm down her spine. Damn Lassiter, she thought, her heart pounding, as she avoided Moran's mocking eyes.

"Now that you've calmed down, just what was today's meeting supposed to prove?"

"It wasn't supposed to prove anything. I only thought it might be fun up there. The two of us."

"Why?"

"It was where my late husband seduced his first wife. It was just a little drama I thought up all by myself."

"And Lassiter had to go and spoil it?"

"Yes, he did. Very much so." And he had, damn him. But not in the way Craig thought.

"You and how many hombres have looked at the view from Pride's Point?"

"That was a disgusting thing to say, Craig."

He laughed.

She felt her cheeks begin to color and looked away, pretending interest in a large buck deer ambling up a steep hillside. The only one aside from Timmie with whom she had been to the point was Dave Ashburn. She had been entranced with the new owner of the Hopeville livery barn and a mild flirtation had turned into a volcanic eruption. It had been a period of living dangerously, especially for her. Doubly so because Ashburn was in Timmie's weekly poker game.

That was why, when Dave Ashburn had been found, shot in the back, she was certain that Timmie had killed him in a jealous rage and not over a losing poker game as everyone thought.

"You didn't answer my question," Moran said mockingly.

"Go to hell." She tried to look him in the eye as they rode through an arch of trees. A cold thought kept nibbling at her. Had Dave Ashburn, before he was killed, talked? She knew that men sometimes did, bragging about the women they'd had.

She realized one thing—she had played her scene today with Lassiter badly. She shouldn't have been so bold and should have shown more shock when Lassiter had told her about Joplin.

"Is it true that Joplin killed my husband?" she asked suddenly.

"Yeah."

"Then why in the world did you hire such a man?"

"Because I can use such a man." The mockery was in his eyes again.

His arrogance was unsettling and made her realize all the more how much she needed Lassiter. Somehow she had to make amends. And one way was to get Craig and the Muleshoe men off his back.

"I lied about Lassiter," she said coolly. "He didn't touch me. I tore my own shirt."

"The damage has been done. If the men catch him, it'll be the rope."

Her face reddened. "Damn it, Craig, I run Muleshoe, not you! I want you to call off the men!"

"I don't like you yelling at me!"

"Then do as you're told!"

"For two cents, I'd blister you. . . ."

"Don't try it, Craig," she warned and fumbled in her saddlebag for the lady's revolver she always carried when she rode.

A flicker of rage began to flame as he watched her,

his face working. But to backhand her would avail him nothing. Plenty of time for discipline once they were married. He took a deep breath and forced a smile.

"I reckon we're both on edge. Sure, I'll call off the boys. Unless they've already found him."

"I doubt if they'd catch Lassiter so easily."

"Probably not."

He left her to ride the rest of the way alone and turned back toward Pride's Point. On the way he debated, hidden by clumps of pines at the base of unscalable canyon walls. Should he hurry and try to intercept Joplin and the others? Or let it alone and later claim he had no luck in finding them?

It was more or less settled for him. He ran into them just leaving the point. It had taken that long for them to hike all the way to the summit and ride down. Joplin was in a foul mood that there had been no sight of Lassiter.

"Just as well," Moran said. "I've changed my mind. Leave him alone . . . for now." Moran looked Joplin over, saw the heft of the big man, the brutality written on his face. "When you get a chance, pick a fight with him. Beat his brains into the ground."

Joplin's wide face split in a grin. "That'd be a pleasure."

When Lassiter felt he had outdistanced any possible pursuers, he cut down through a long valley until he saw a small house ahead, Bert Stencoe's old place. He was about to ride on by when he noticed smoke curling from the tin chimney. Riding up, he reined in and yelled, "Hello in the house!"

A slim figure came to the porch. It was Ellen Stencoe, wearing a shirt and boy's Levis. She held a double-barreled shotgun.

"What do you want?" she asked coldly.

"Just happened by. I thought maybe you'd invite me in for coffee."

She debated, frowning. Her dark hair was pulled back, held at the back of her neck with a green ribbon. "Come on in. I want to talk to you, anyway."

He'd been in the place several times when her brother was alive. He had been a gruff, unsociable man but for some reason he and Timmie Borling had hit it off. Ellen heated coffee and filled two cups. She had pulled up an extra chair and across the seat of this she placed the shotgun.

Lassiter smiled. "Don't be afraid of me."

"I'm not, just cautious." She glanced at the shotgun. "The sheriff turned it over to me. He said it had belonged to my brother. It . . . it's the one he's supposed to have used when he killed himself." She sighed, blowing out her cheeks, and stared at the floor covered only by a rather ragged Indian rug.

"I hope you still don't think I had anything to do with it," Lassiter said after a drawn-out silence.

"Half of the people in town, they stick up for you. The other half . . ." She spread her shapely hands. "You know how it is, I guess."

"Half for, half against. Sure, I know how it is." Seen in daylight she was quite attractive, the eyes large and soulful, the lips full and moist.

"There's talk in town that my brother was . . . was a cow thief."

Lassiter sipped coffee while thinking of a reply. The

coffee was bitter but hot. He kept one eye on the front window, which gave him a good view down sloping tracks to the main road. A rafter at the end of the porch caught his eye. A yellow rope was tied to the end where it projected over the edge of the porch. About two feet of it dangled in the breeze, the rest had evidently been hacked off with a knife.

"Every nester now and then slow elks a neighbor's beef," Lassiter said, choosing his words. "Borling didn't mind your brother eating Muleshoe beef."

"But that's no reason to call him a thief."

"Where'd you hear this talk of thief?"

"At the store in town. Some women were talking. When they noticed me nearby they shut up. It was not only embarrassing, it hurt me deeply to hear such talk about my brother."

"I can imagine."

"When he came back from the war our parents were dead and I was a little tyke living with an aunt. My brother kept us going until he could no longer work. By then I had a job teaching school in Tucson. Thinking the mountains would be good for his health, he came up here." She gave a long sigh. "He was wounded in the war. A bullet in one lung."

"I remember he coughed a lot. You still think I had anything to do with his death?"

She shook her head. "I had a long talk with the sheriff. He assured me you weren't guilty."

"Sloan sticking up for me? I'll be damned."

"But he insists my brother killed Dave Ashburn then wrote out a confession and shot himself."

He drained the last of the coffee. She said the pot

was empty but she would make more. He shook his head.

"You sure it's wise you staying out here alone?"

She smiled; her teeth were large and white. She patted the shotgun on the chair beside her. "Nobody's going to bother me."

"Just the same . . ." He tried to talk her into taking a room at the hotel until she left town. But she said she couldn't afford it, for one thing.

"Ralph wants his own place before we're married," she explained. "We're putting aside every dollar we can spare. I shouldn't have spent the money to come up here. But I felt I just had to try and clear my brother's name."

"Tell me about this Ralph," he suggested to take her mind óff her brother.

"I've known him most of my life." She said that Ralph Benson had gone to work for the Tyburn Cattle Company at fourteen and gradually worked his way up to *segundo*. "He knows the cattle business and I know he'll be a success with his own ranch."

Lassiter rubbed the side of his face and sighed. "I was *segundo* at Muleshoe but it didn't make me rich."

"Maybe you just lack Ralph's burning ambition."

He laughed. "Probably. I'm a drifter at heart."

She thrust out her hand. "If I don't see you again, Mr. Lassiter, I want you to know it's been a pleasure. And I regret the things I said about you. . . ."

He clasped her hand. Her grip was firm, but the hand soft and warm. Somehow, touching her flesh put a tingle along his spine. And as he stared down into her attractive face, the lips slowly parted and the eyes grew round and began to tear. Her mouth began to tremble and suddenly the tears came. Lassiter brought his arms around her. He could feel the hot tears through the front of his shirt. Picking her up, he carried her to a battered sofa and sat her down. He sat beside her, an arm over her shoulders, her head tight against his chest. Birds in the trees beyond the porch seemed startled by the sounds of her sobbing. They swooped into the air, chattering, and came back to the sheltering branches.

At last the sobs began to subside and she no longer trembled against him. Finally, she sat up and dabbed at her eyes with a small handkerchief. Then she drew back to peer up into his face.

"I guess I had that coming," she said in a muffled voice. "It's the first time I've really let go since hearing about my brother."

"It's a good thing to let off steam."

"I guess the touch of your hand . . . I don't know, but it seemed to do something to me." She drew a deep breath, frowning as if baffled.

Again he tried to get her to go to town, but she wanted a few more days at her brother's nester spread.

"If you need help, you know where to yell," he said with a smile. Then he bent his head and kissed her gently. Her lips tasted salty from tears.

As he mounted up, she was still standing on the small porch, a startled look on her face. When he was down at the road, he looked back to see her in the doorway, her hand lifted. He waved to her, then rode on.

In town, he hunted up Jim Sloan and found the sheriff just about to close up his office for the day. "You still around?" he grunted, giving Lassiter a sidelong glance.

"I want to thank you, Jim, for putting in a good word for me with Ellen Stencoe."

Sloan stood in the center of his cluttered office with desk and chairs and a table. "Told her the truth, that you had nothin' to do with what happened to her brother."

"One thing bothers me, Jim. Stencoe writing out a confession, then killing himself."

Sloan started to color, then looked angry. "You oughta be damn glad he did, Lassiter. Or you'd still be sweatin' out the years down at Rimshaw."

"Who really killed Dave Ashburn? I'm damn sure you know Timmie and I didn't do it."

"Will you leave well enough alone, for Christ's sake? I'm sorry you ever came back here, Lassiter. I figured once you got out, you'd quit this territory faster'n a streak of lightning."

"I came back mainly because of Borling's son. And now I find out that Joplin's here."

"The bug cuss that Moran hired on." Sloan rubbed his jaw.

"He killed Timmie. Right in front of my eyes." Lassiter's voice hardened. "I'm gonna get that bastard . . ."

"Don't blame you none if what you say is true."

"Damn right it's true. I was *there!*"

Sloan got Lassiter by an arm. "Let's take a walk. No tellin' who's got an ear to the door."

Lassiter waited until Sloan lowered the window shade, locked the front door, then came shuffling along the walk. In the silence they both rolled cigarettes. Lassiter scraped a match alight and they halted to fire up.

"I'll tell you why I'm sorry you came back, Lassiter," Sloan said as they were walking out through shadowed trees at the edge of town. "You've got a way with the ladies."

"Just what in hell is that supposed to mean?"

"I got my eye on Delira Borling. I purely ache just thinkin' about that woman. Even when she was married to Timmie I . . . I loved her. But I knowed then nothin' could ever come of it."

A hard suspicion began to take shape in Lassiter's mind.

"I know what you're thinkin'," Sloan said quickly, turning his head to stare at Lassiter. "I didn't frame you two so's I could get Timmie's wife. No, I never done that. I couldn't do a thing that low. At first it was Craig Moran she was all lah-dee-dah about, but lately I notice she's cooled off toward him."

"So?"

"An' now you come back into the picture. She'll turn to you, sure as hell. An' I wanted to be the one she'd ask for help."

They walked a dozen yards in silence, their boots stepping softly over layers of pine needles.

"She's a widow now and fair game. Jim, why not present your case? You've got as much chance as anybody."

"Not with you hangin' around."

"I don't care much for the lady."

"I seen the way she looked at you the night of the school dance."

"As long as we're talking, who do you think killed Dave Ashburn?"

The sheriff was silent for so long that Lassiter began to believe he hadn't heard him.

"I'm sayin' this for your ears alone, Lassiter," Sloan said soberly. "I think Moran killed him."

"You must have some proof," Lassiter said narrowly.

"Not a smidgin."

"Then what the hell . . ."

"Just a hunch. Pure hunch. You recollect when Ashburn came here an' bought the livery stable?"

"Sure, I remember."

"Pocket bulgin' with money. Bought everybody drinks. Wrangled his way into them poker games Borling used to have once a week."

"Yeah, but what's that got to do with Moran killing him?"

"Moran showed up here one day. I caught him an' Ashburn glarin' at each other a few times. They'd been arguin' but when I came up they broke off. Once I overheard Moran say somethin' about money owed him. Next thing I know, Ashburn's shot in the back an' your names are in the dust, yours an' Timmie Borling's. Lookin' like Ashburn wrote 'em with his last breath."

"A man shot in the back doesn't do much writing."

"It's what I tried to tell the judge, but he wouldn't listen. A lot of folks around here have got it in for Muleshoe on account of it bein' the biggest spread in these parts. Most everybody wanted a quick trial. Which they got."

"Amen."

The sheriff halted. "Let's walk back. It's supper-time. Buy you a steak. If I got your promise to head for new frontiers."

"Sorry, Jim, I'm sticking."

"I aim to ask Delira to marry with me. An' that'll take care of the boy. You got my word on it," said the sheriff.

They started back. Windows were beginning to blossom with yellow lamplight. A half moon hung low on the horizon and the first stars were still competing with lingering daylight.

"Didn't you hear what I said about the boy?" Sloan asked.

"I heard."

"Then do I buy you that steak?"

"Not if you expect me to leave town."

"Stubborn cuss, ain't you?"

"Been known to be. There's more to the Bert Stencoe business than you told me. Am I right?"

"Yep."

"Then tell me the rest of it."

"I got business up at the capital. Be gone most of a week. When I get back we'll have a talk."

That was all Lassiter could get out of him.

# Chapter Nine

The following day, in shadows by the schoolyard, Lassiter called out softly to the boy. "Rance . . ."

The kid had been brooding, kicking at stones as he walked home. He carried two books in a strap slung over a narrow shoulder. Upon hearing Lassiter's voice, his small face brightened and he dashed into the clump of trees where Lassiter was crouched. Small arms were flung around Lassiter's neck.

"When you came to the house," Rance said, panting, "I couldn't say anything. 'Cause old man Adderly was right behind me."

"I figured something like that. How're they treating you, anyhow?"

"Terrible." Rance Borling hastened to explain in detail his treatment by the Adderlys. "I want to live at the ranch, but Delira won't let me." He seemed close to tears, the large eyes, so reminiscent of his father, turned up to Lassiter's grim face.

Taking Rance by the hand, Lassiter stood up and started with him toward Hopeville's business district.

Smoke from cook fires already stained the late afternoon sky. Birds chattered in tall trees that lined the street. A freight outfit, mule bells tinkling, came grinding up the grade into town.

Lassiter knew there was nothing legal he could do about changing the boy's situation; after all, Delira was his stepmother, his guardian. But in the future changes would be made. He walked with Rance to the Adderly house.

"You won't have to stay here long, Rance," Lassiter assured him. "Just long enough for me to straighten out a few things."

This meant handling Joplin for the cold-blooded murder of the boy's father. And to pursue Jim Sloan's theory that Moran and Dave Ashburn had had money dealings somewhere other than Hopeville, that Moran had demanded a settlement which Ashburn failed to acknowledge. So Moran had killed him. And, seeing a chance to move in at Muleshoe, had pinned the blame on Borling and Lassiter.

The boy entered the Adderly house by the rear door that was left unlocked for him. On his heels was Lassiter. The balloon-shaped Mrs. Adderly was beating dough in a bowl and turned white at the sight of Lassiter. Her husband was snoring on the sofa.

"Mike!" she screamed.

Mike Adderly snorted, sat up, blinking. He was a large, red-eyed man with tousled hair and a missing front tooth.

He glared at Lassiter, but something in Lassiter's eyes caused him to swallow and lower his gaze.

"I don't want either one of you to lay a hand on this

boy again," Lassiter said coldly. "Treat him like a star boarder. Otherwise I'll be back."

Neither of the Adderlys said anything. Lassiter gave Rance a pat on the shoulder and left the house.

He walked through growing shadows toward the main street. As he passed the wagon yard adjoining the stable, he wondered who had taken it over after Dave Ashburn was killed. In some way he had to trap Moran and get the truth out of him. While he was mulling over the many possibilities, he saw Ellen Stencoe start to pull out of the wagon yard in a spring wagon. A smile appeared on her attractive face as she saw him. She pulled up the team.

"Where in the world have you been?" she asked. "I was in town all day yesterday. . . ."

"Had things to do." He didn't explain that he had waited out near Muleshoe headquarters, hoping for sight of Joplin. But he hadn't seen the man so had come into town.

"I came in for a few odds and ends." She gestured at supplies in the wagon bed, things she had picked up at the Mercantile. "I'm leaving the end of the week, going back to Tucson."

He glanced at the sky. "You won't get home before dark."

"I'm afraid not."

"Could be dangerous. I'll get my horse and ride out with you."

"I'll be quite all right."

"Or you stay the night here in the hotel and I'll ride out with you in the morning."

She started to smile, then her mouth froze, the eyes round and terrified.

It was all the warning Lassiter needed. As he spun around, she screamed. Just as he reached for his gun, something struck him a tremendous blow behind the right ear. The force of the blow drove light from his brain and in the sudden darkness he collapsed to his knees.

Men from the stable stopped what they were doing and began to shout and come at a run. "Fight!" one of them yelled.

Almost instantly, dim consciousness returned to Lassiter and he saw a man standing over him, rubbing the knuckles of his clenched right fist. Ellen Stencoe was crying out in protest and at the same time trying to hold in her skittish team that was on edge because of the shouting, then the sudden rush of men. The whites of their eyes showed as the screams and yells increased.

On hands and knees, Lassiter vaguely saw a boot toe kick out to catch him a stunning smash in the ribs. Pain ripped through him as he was flopped over on his back.

"He'll kill him!" Lassiter heard Ellen Stencoe scream.

And then in his numbness he looked up past a pair of thick legs into the triumphant grin of Meager Joplin.

"Give 'em room, give 'em room!" a man was shouting.

"It isn't fair!" Ellen cried. "He was struck down when his back was turned."

Her protest, however, was barely heard above the noisy excitement. What was coming was something to savor, a break in the monotony of frontier life where the only entertainment was an occasional medicine show or a threadbare theatrical troupe who performed at the schoolhouse.

Joplin, looming huge in the gathering twilight, was enjoying the moment.

"Have at him, big fella!" a bearded man shouted at Joplin. "He used to be *segundo* for Muleshoe. I hate Muleshoe's guts!" The man didn't realize that Joplin drew pay from the big cattle outfit.

It brought a laugh from Joplin. Believing he had all the time in the world, he leisurely drew back his right foot, ready to unleash it against Lassiter's unprotected face. But as he moved, Lassiter suddenly came to life. Both arms were abruptly wrapped around Joplin's left leg, pulling him down beside Lassiter. This brought on a new chorus of yells erupting from the growing crowd.

Somehow in those moments, Lassiter regained his feet. The street seemed tilted, the onlookers in danger of sliding off into oblivion. He reached for his gun, intending to end this before it could go any further. He had no intention of fighting the giant Joplin and running the risk of ending up a cripple. Or dead.

Many large men frequently have ponderous movements. Not so with Joplin. He leaped to his feet, his yellowish eyes showing pleasure. Lassiter was still fumbling for his gun, only then realizing the holster was empty. He looked around to see if it had fallen when he went down. Joplin hit him a glancing blow on the jaw, as Lassiter was able to pull his chin aside at the last moment. But there still was sufficient power to slam him against a rear wheel of Ellen Stencoe's wagon.

The jolt caused her nervous team to lunge into their collars. Lassiter was clutching at the wheel rim for support when it suddenly began to turn, burning the palms of his hands. He was knocked backward into the crowd. Somebody caught him under the arms.

"Runaway!" someone screamed as Ellen Stencoe and her team went sailing down the street, scattering pedestrians.

Lassiter's heart turned cold and despite the numbness that gripped most of his body, he managed to shout, "Somebody help her!"

Joplin pulled off his hat and sailed it into the crowd, then came toward Lassiter, his hands wide from his body, teeth bared. At each of Joplin's advancing steps, Lassiter backed away. Joplin began to come for him at a loping run that Lassiter copied in his backward flight.

"Stand still an' fight!" Joplin screeched. "By Christ, I was told to put your brains in the dust an' by God I will!"

His chest began to heave from the exertion of trying to outmaneuver Lassiter, who still backed, then circled. Joplin was doggedly at his footsteps. Others were beginning to take up the chant for Lassiter to stand his ground and fight like a man.

Two blocks away Ellen Stencoe finally began to slow the team down by leaning her full weight back on the lines. But the spring wagon was bouncing over the ruts at times in danger of overturning and spilling her out. Some of her supplies had already been flung from the wagon.

Just as she brought the team to a halt, two men on horseback came spurring up, the thinner of the pair shouting, "We figured you was a goner."

"A fine piece of drivin' you done, ma'am!" yelled his chunky companion.

"Help me rescue Lassiter from that awful man!" she cried.

Both men shook their heads. "It's a fair fight an' we got to git back to it."

Turning their horses, they spurred back to the scene of the fight. Just as they sprang from the saddle, Lassiter's head finally cleared. He stood his ground suddenly as the crowd had been yelling for him to do.

He seemed on the point of taking Joplin's rush head on. But at the last minute he twisted aside. And as Joplin tried to recover, he sank lefts and rights into his rib cage.

"*Aaaaaahhhhhhhh!*" Joplin groaned. He hugged himself, his eyes murderous. A glancing blow to the temple snapped Joplin's head back.

"All right, you son of a bitch!" Joplin snarled through his teeth. Bending down, the fingers of his right hand closed over the handle of a weapon he had hidden in his boot. Out came a Bowie knife with six inches of glittering blade. The crowd gasped and fell back.

"Ain't fair!" a man yelled at Joplin, but no one moved to try and take the knife away from him. At that moment a knife landed in the dust at Lassiter's feet with a dull plop. Keeping his eyes on Joplin, Lassiter slowly stooped and picked it up.

Who had thrown him the knife? He had no idea. But it put him even with Joplin, who was grinning now, stamping his feet like a rutting bull.

"You bleed easy?" he taunted. "We'll soon see."

That Joplin knew his business with a knife was evident from the first, for he assumed the stance of a swordsman, his thick fingers curled around the hilt so that the blade was a lethal extension of his arm. He didn't hold it overhead to bring it down in chopping strokes like an amateur.

Joplin lunged and the blades made a rasping sound as they came together. Quickly they broke apart. At first the crowd was silent as if aware of the awesome potential represented by the knives. Before, it had been a matter of fists only. A man's blood could flow on the ground but the outcome wasn't necessarily lethal. With the twin savage blades the ending could be death. And they seemed to know it.

As Lassiter parried and struck, the point of his knife made an X across the front of Joplin's shirt. Droplets of blood appeared through the severed fabric. Joplin winced, grinding his teeth, obviously in pain.

But all Lassiter could think of was Timmie Borling fleeing through the mesquite along the river and shot in the back. Killed by this giant of a man now dancing about, his teeth bared, making swiping motions in the air with his knife.

This time when the blades came together they

clanged, the sound carrying off into the trees and lost in the uproar that burst from the crowd.

Joplin feinted at the midsection and as Lassiter lowered his guard to counter, the knife shifted toward his eyes, making a swiping motion that could have blinded him had it connected. But Lassiter danced backwards and then closed. Their right arms locked together, their faces inches apart. Lassiter could feel the hot air from Joplin's heavy breathing against his face. There was an odor of whiskey on the breath.

"You're dead, Lassiter," Joplin hissed. "Take a look . . . it's the last sun you'll ever see."

Not that there was much of the sun left to see anyway. It had slid far to the west to turn the sky pinkish and yellow. Shadows lengthened under the trees that bordered the wagon yard.

Finally, Lassiter got his arm unlocked and thrust Joplin back and jumped aside, escaping the tip of the blade that was aimed at his groin by inches.

At a crouch, he stalked the bigger man, moving first to the right, then the left. Their blades rasped and clanged, depending on how hard they came together. Joplin, still grinning, expertly matched his every move. Shaggy brown hair curved on either side of his sweaty face.

While trying to twist aside, Lassiter's boot came down on a stone that rolled with him. He was thrown to one knee and as he went down, the tip of Joplin's blade lashed his cheek. He felt the warmth of blood flow down the side of his face, to his neck, soaking into the collar of his shirt. A woman's scream cut through the shouting males. He thought it was Ellen Stencoe but he couldn't be sure. He leaped to his feet.

"That was only a sample," Joplin said through his teeth as they closed again. They wrestled, each gripping the other's knife wrist with the free hand, the blades inches from each other's chest. Joplin had not lost any of his bull-like strength and was able to wrestle Lassiter off his feet. But after a few stumbling steps, Lassiter came down solidly. He pulled in his stomach as Joplin slashed at it. The knife blade winked in the fading light.

They came together, broke apart, circling, dancing away to escape the lethal steel. By now, Joplin's powerful chest was bared because the slashed shirt hung around his belt like a lowered flag. Impatiently, he tore it free. The X cut through the chest hair by the point of Lassiter's knife was bleeding.

The pain of Lassiter's lacerated cheek was dimmed by his hatred of the big man before him. In the twilight, Joplin assumed the look of a large bear with a bloodied chest, hair ragged on his head. They lunged, parried, thrust and cut the air with their blades instead of human flesh. But Lassiter knew and so did the onlookers that it couldn't continue this way for long. Soon one of them would make a mistake and then death's somber wings would raise dust in the Hopeville wagon yard.

Watching for his chance, Lassiter led Joplin into trying for his exposed chest. But at the last moment he danced back. It left Joplin leaning far over, his arm extended. Without losing a beat, Lassiter swung in close and brought the butt of his knife down hard on Joplin's right wrist. Joplin gave a yelp of pain and dropped his knife. It lay glittering in the dust. Before he could retrieve it, however, the knife was covered by Lassiter's foot.

A gasp went up from the crowd as Lassiter said, "By rights I could kill you."

"You ain't got the guts."

"You're right. I couldn't kill you in cold blood as you did Timmie Borling."

It brought an exclamation from the onlookers because most of them were unaware of Joplin's hand in Borling's death.

Drawing back his foot, Lassiter kicked the knife across the ground into the crowd. Then he threw his own knife after it.

"We'll finish as we started it," Lassiter snarled, lifting his fists.

Hardly were the words out of Lassiter's mouth when Joplin charged. His fist swung at the cut on Lassiter's cheek, connecting. Lassiter went stumbling backwards, a roaring Joplin in pursuit. Head down, powerful arms flailing, Joplin pursued him relentlessly. But Lassiter kept back, the crowd giving way behind him at each move, people stumbling to get out of the way.

Once as he whirled he glimpsed Ellen Stencoe, her eyes round in a face gone dead white. And in that moment he took a terrible smash to the shoulder that spun him. Thinking he had Lassiter on the verge of defeat, Joplin came roaring in to finish it. But Lassiter's left straightened him up from his crouched position. And before he could come down from his toes to heels,

Lassiter drove a right into the center of the nose. That brought a scream of pain and rage. Joplin backed quickly, his nose a bloodied nub of flesh in the center of his face.

Screeching, Joplin charged like an enraged bull, crashing into Lassiter with such force he was driven back into the crowd. Willing hands kept him on his feet, and pushed him back.

"You got him on the run, Lassiter!" one man yelled.

It was not true, for Lassiter was far from having Joplin on the run. But he knew one thing: He could no longer let his fury at this man's hand in Timmie Borling's death make him reckless. Therefore, he took a half-minute of evasive action, keeping out of Joplin's reach as the man's broad fists whistled through the air around him.

Watching for his chance, Lassiter feinted with his right, whipped a left into Joplin's solar plexus. Then, as the man involuntarily leaned forward like a great tree about to topple, Lassiter leveled him with his right to the jaw.

A great shout erupted from the crowd as Joplin fell loosely like a rolled-up carpet.

"You done it, Lassiter!" a man yelled, whacking him on the back. "You beat the big bastard, you did!"

The cry was taken up by others.

Lassiter was dabbing a bandanna against the laceration on his cheek. It hurt, when he tried to grin at the crowd, to show his appreciation for their support. At first, the majority had been against him but his valiant stand against a much larger man had won them over.

For the first time he saw Craig Moran standing

alone by a line of rigs being stored in the wagon yard. His handsome face wore an ugly smile. He lifted a hand to the abrasion on his cheek where the skin had been broken by Lassiter's knuckles the night of the school dance.

"Seems you got some of the same," Moran said, nodding at Lassiter's bloodied cheek. "Too bad it couldn't have been your throat."

People nearby turned their heads to stare. There was a sudden silence.

"Keep Joplin away from me," Lassiter said coldly. "I aim to settle with him for murdering Timmie Borling. Seems today wasn't the time."

"If you got an ounce of brains, you'll get the hell out while you can still breathe," Moran said thinly.

A lank man hobbling on a makeshift crutch came to stand at Moran's side. It was the man Lassiter had shot down at Lew Oliver's inn at the Crossroads and who had disappeared.

# Chapter Ten

"I hope you stay around, Lassiter," Petey Sagar said with a vicious smile. "I owe you for puttin' a bullet in me. An' for killin' my brother Rupe."

"That's enough, Petey," Moran said, jerking his head for silence. "Some of you Muleshoe men see if you can get Joplin on his feet."

A half-dozen of them materialized from the shadows. By now, Joplin was beginning to snort and roll about on the ground, his yellowish eyes glazed, his mouth hanging open. Dried blood from his smashed nose and a deep cut on his jaw stained his face.

Ellen Stencoe came up then, breathing deeply, shaking her head from side to side. She gripped Lassiter by the arms. "Lassiter, Lassiter," she said in a weak voice, "you scared me half to death."

"If you still insist on going home, I'm riding with you," he announced. "No telling what might happen now."

He drove her wagon to where he had left his horse,

tied the mount to the tailgate then climbed back to the seat and picked up the reins.

"Why in the world do you think anything could happen to me?" she asked when they were driving out of town.

"For one thing, your brother's place is on Muleshoe land."

"It is? You sure about that?"

"Dead sure." Then he caught himself, hating his use of the word "dead." He told her calmly that from time to time nesters squatted on the fringes of the big outfits. Usually they didn't last long.

"But as I told you, Timmie Borling took a liking to your brother. Maybe because he was a wounded soldier, I don't know. He never said. But he let him stay and gave orders to leave him alone."

"That was nice of him."

"Timmie was that way with folks he liked."

The only sounds were the clatter of the wagon, the click of shod hooves on an occasional rock as he drove north out of town. The moon had climbed and brightened. Only a trace of roseate sunset remained on the far western horizon. Soon the sky would be shot full of stars.

"You scared the hell out of me when your team ran away," Lassiter said as the road steepened and curved through clumps of pines and juniper.

"I remembered what Ralph always told me if it ever happened. To keep my head, above all, and not to panic and jump."

"Good advice from this Ralph of yours. You bring the shotgun to town with you?"

She nodded, her hair soft against his neck. "It's in the back."

"Good."

He was scanning both sides of the road, frowning at the pools of shadow. What a place for an ambush, he thought.

"Maybe you better get it," he suggested. "The shotgun."

He slowed the team and she turned in the seat and leaned back. She brought it up with one hand, then said a little anxiously, "Do you think there might be trouble?"

To the west a last finger of daylight lingered at a high canyon rim while below everything was in shade. By the time they reached the Stencoe place the sky was strewn with glittering stars.

There was a whir of insects as he put up the team. Ellen went indoors. He washed his hands and face in a shallow stream that flowed past the house, noticing an aroma of cooking bacon. While waiting for it to cook, Ellen got arnica, which she applied to the cut on his cheek. Her fingers were warm and gentle.

"Thank goodness it isn't any worse," she said with a shake of her head. "It could have been your eye."

"He tried hard enough."

After a supper of bacon and flapjacks and strong coffee he felt better. But he was still bruised and his cheek burned like fire. She had cooked in the dark, since he suggested not lighting a lamp. "Somebody might make a try for me," he said half in jest, "and hit you by mistake."

They talked in the dark for an hour or more and he learned about her life in detail. Especially about her betrothed, Ralph Benson, with his ambition to own his own spread. It would take years of scrimping and saving on a *segundo*'s pay to buy a ranch the size he wanted.

"Ralph wants it before we're married," Ellen said softly in the darkness. "And so do I," she added with a deep sigh.

"Life's too damn short, Ellen. If you care for each other, get married now. Worry about the rest of it later."

"Have you ever settled down to marry?"

"No, but that's got nothing to do with it."

"You expect me to follow your advice, yet you won't accept it yourself." She laughed softly.

"Cattle ranching is a tough game. Maybe you can talk Ralph into trying something easier."

"He doesn't want something easier. He's a hard worker and has this one ambition. And I believe he's going to make it."

Lassiter started to mention the odds against it, then decided to keep his mouth shut. He yawned, started to get up. "I'll bunk in the shed."

"Nonsense, you'll bunk here. I'll sleep on the sofa and you can have the bed."

"If there's going to be any of that, I'll take the sofa."

By accident their hands met in the darkness. Then their lips. Not a word was said but it seemed perfectly natural when they shared the big bed formerly occupied by her brother, the late Bert Stencoe.

And when she had taken the bold step, she knew that she was in love. Somehow she'd tame this black-eyed hellion and get him to settle down. All he had needed was the right woman to show him the way. And it had come to her suddenly that she was that woman.

In the first grayish streamers of dawn, he opened his eyes, not remembering where he was at first. The right side of his face was stiff and sore from the knife cut on his cheek.

"Good morning." It was a girl's voice and he turned his head, remembering. She was smiling, dark hair loose about her face, the eyes filled with mischief.

He knew he should say something to reassure her, but in the cold light of dawn he sensed he had made a mistake. But it was too late now for regrets. Last night everything had fallen so easily into place, as if preordained. Reaching out, he smoothed the hair back from her face. In the faint light she looked vibrant.

His months away from women at Rimshaw Prison had left a monumental need which wouldn't be satisfied with one encounter. And would once more do any more damage than had already been done? he asked himself.

For so long his life had been tenuous; at any time he could have been beaten to death by one of the guards. It occurred less frequently, he had been told, under Galendor's regime, but it still happened.

And there was always the chance that if he did make a break, the Gatling gun up on the guard tower would start ratcheting explosions before he could get very far and stitch him with bullets faster than he could blink.

Even after gaining his freedom, he had played fast and loose with his life. Entering Paco's and grabbing the girl, he was so filled with hatred for those who had framed Timmie Borling and himself that he lost his reason. The towering barkeep, Barney, could as easily have lifted a sawed-off shotgun from behind his bar and blown him out the front door.

Later, at the Crossroads, there had been two of them. The Sagar brothers, Lew Oliver said they called themselves, Rupe and Petey. If the pair had coordinated their attack better, he might not now be lying in a warm bed in a nester shack at the edge of Muleshoe Ranch with an attractive young lady.

Make the most of the moment, Lassiter told himself. And he did, bringing her to a point where her muffled scream, her lips against his throat, streaked through the morning stillness.

She hummed as she cooked breakfast while he went to feed the livestock. By now the sun had climbed until it shone brightly through the great stand of pines to the east of the house. He was just forking hay into the corral when something struck one of the tines, a shock which he felt clear to his shoulders. Even before he heard the sharp explosion of a rifle, he knew he was a target. He had worn his gun, thank God.

Dropping the pitchfork, he crouched low behind the milling horses and started for the house at a run, gun in hand.

"Keep down, Ellen!" he shouted.

Another rifle opened up from the opposite direction, making a great *thonk* as its bullet drilled a knothole in a pine a few feet to his right. He flung himself down and rolled against a trough. The first rifleman spotted him and sent a bullet close to his face and a second into the wooden wall of the trough. Water leaked through the bullethole and ran under the trough and down a slant so that it soaked his pants leg. Cold, but it's better than my blood, was the thought that shot through his mind as once again he was on his feet, sprinting for the house. Both rifles opened up. Knowing that he would only draw fire to Ellen, he veered for the ramshackle barn, ran clear through the musty structure and out a rear door where he surprised a bearded man. The man was standing up with his rifle raised in a circle of large rocks, looking toward the house.

Lassiter remembered him vaguely as being with the Muleshoe men at the wagon yard yesterday. Through the unbuttoned neck of the man's checkered shirt a tuft of chest hair protruded. It seemed by the sound that they fired simultaneously. Only Lassiter's shot was a shade before the stranger's. For an instant it seemed that the man was suspended in the air. Then the rifle went flying, clattering onto the rocks where he had been hidden. And then the man, all limp-legged, followed it down.

"Petey, he got Max!" came a yell from up the slope in the trees. This was followed by the explosion of a rifle. A bullet whanged off one of the large rocks. Lassiter leaped the barricade and came down beside the man he had shot. The man's eyes were closed and he was breathing heavily. Blood bubbled from a wound high in his chest.

Lassiter tossed away the man's rifle but did not have

109

time to go through his clothing to look for additional weapons. The other two men were opening up their fire now, bullets slamming into the stone barricade, screaming as they ricocheted away. All Lassiter could see of one man was a puff of smoke far up in the trees on a slope to one side of the house; the other man he couldn't see at all.

He aimed at the smoke and fired, hoping his .44 would carry the distance. It produced a scream, then silence. His mouth was dry as he waited anxiously.

Something made him look around. The bearded man had somehow managed to pull a revolver from under his shirt. Lassiter saw it big as a cannon pointed at his head, the man laboriously drawing back the hammer. Since he was too far to try and grab the gun, Lassiter shot him. The man's head twitched and he fired into the ground and fell dead across the revolver.

Far to the west of the house he could hear a horse at a walk, moving away. And as Lassiter listened, its rider kicked it into a gallop, the sounds fading swiftly.

Then Lassiter went cautiously up the slope to check on the other rifleman who had been hidden in the trees. The man lay on his back, his legs at a sprawl. Lassiter pulled up the man's shirt to expose a hairy belly and ugly hole the bullet had made in his stomach. From the twisted features, Lassiter guessed he had died in agony.

But Lassiter felt no sympathy for either man. When he ran back to the house he found Ellen standing in the middle of the room, gripping the shotgun. The sight of Lassiter brought tears to her eyes, which began spilling down her cheeks. She ran to him. Lassiter took away the shotgun while her arms came around him in a frantic embrace.

"I was so frightened for you, Lassiter," she sobbed.

But she soon recovered and went ahead with the breakfast she had been cooking before the gunfire started.

While he was eating he thought of the one who had gotten away. Petey, someone had called him. Obviously, Petey Sagar would live to try his ambush another day.

# Chapter Eleven

That incredible Lassiter luck. Moran had heard about it, but disbelieved it. No man could be that lucky. But here it was, the proof of it once again. First, there had been the business at Rimshaw Prison, Timmie Borling getting killed, but Lassiter surviving only because the prison superintendent had taken it into his head to ride that morning down through the prison cotton fields. Then at the Crossroads, two good men were sent to intercept him and once again Lassiter escaped unscathed, but Rupe Sagar was dead.

And now it was more of the same. Last night Moran had seen Lassiter and the Stencoe girl leave town together. That meant they'd spend the night at the nester place. All right, it would make things easier. Ever since his return from the Crossroads, Petey Sagar had been gnashing his teeth in a desire to get even with Lassiter for what had happened to his brother.

Moran had called Sagar into the ranch office, which adjoined his foreman quarters at Muleshoe. "You want Lassiter so bad, here's your chance."

"Do I want him." Petey Sagar bared his teeth.

"Take Max and Louie with you. Be out at the Stencoe place by dawn. The three of you spread out. Lassiter is bound to come out of the house. When he does, get him."

"He's as good as dead, Craig."

Moran stiffened at the man's use of his first name, but decided to let it ride for the present.

But just half an hour ago, Sagar had come in, flogging a weary horse and apparently badly shaken. Lassiter hadn't been alone out at the Stencoe place, Sagar reported.

"There was three hombres with Lassiter, maybe four. They opened up on us afore we could get set. Louie an' Max, they got it right off. I didn't stand no chance against so many so I hightailed it."

Moran cut him off with his lifted hand. He suspected some of it to be a lie. But one thing for sure, it was the old Lassiter luck once again.

With the sheriff still at the territorial capital on business of some kind, Moran knew he should act fast. He was surprised that Sloan hadn't appointed a deputy before leaving as he usually did when going out of town. Maybe he forgot, Moran reasoned, or perhaps he'd done it deliberately, hoping some of the mess would be cleaned up without benefit of the law, before he returned.

He didn't trust Sloan. Many times he'd noticed the sheriff giving him sidelong glances and when Moran would look around, the sheriff would pretend his attention was elsewhere.

In the back of Moran's mind lurked the possibility

that Sloan knew more about the Ashburn killing than he let on. When Moran, after many months, had finally tracked Ashburn down, after the bastard ran out on him, following their cattle deal in Chihuahua City, he had tried to get him to settle up. But Ashburn claimed he had put all his spare cash into the livery stable he had purchased in Hopeville. Moran called him a liar. They were about to come to blows or worse when Sloan happened along. The sheriff pretended he hadn't overheard the argument. But had he?

By that time Moran had become the target of the flirtatious Mrs. Timothy Borling. It was Ashburn who had bragged about her first, relating the times he'd been with her up at Pride's Point while her husband was away at roundup.

But Ashburn had the mind of a common thief, proved when he had run off with their funds from the cattle sale, hoping to settle comfortably in a new territory. Patiently, Moran had tracked him down. Ashburn lacked any creativity in his makeup; his philosophy being to grab what was in sight. Such as the cattle money. Such as Delira Borling.

Moran, on the other hand, saw a future. Mrs. Borling liked him; she had proven that, finally. With her husband out of the way, along with his sidekick Lassiter, new avenues would open up.

He had stalked Dave Ashburn after the poker game, shot him in the back, then scratched the names of Borling and Lassiter into the dust.

At the Trail's End he had used his considerable oratorical talents to whip the citizenry into a froth to avenge the death of the new owner of their livery stable. Disappointed that Borling and Lassiter weren't sentenced to hang, Moran eventually made other plans.

Moran, sitting on the edge of his desk in the ranch office, eyed Petey Sagar, who was elaborating on the morning's disaster. On this newer version, there were definitely four men with Lassiter instead of three.

"How's your leg?" Moran inquired when Sagar had finished.

"Still a little stiff, but I get around."

"That you do, Petey." Lassiter's bullet down at the Crossroads had cut an ugly slash across Petey's upper thigh. Moran called Joplin into the office and told the pair he had a job for them.

While they waited for details, he walked up through the trees to the big house and entered without bothering to knock. Senna showed her disapproval, then walked flat-footed back to the kitchen. One more sore point Moran intended to get rid of just as soon as he and Delira were married. And yesterday he had given her an ultimatum; the day after tomorrow they would wed.

But with his new plans, the wedding probably should be postponed a week. Because of the boy. There would be a great hue and cry raised, of course, and they probably shouldn't get married so close to the tragedy.

He took the stairs two at a time and entered Delira's bedroom. She was sitting on a flimsy chair brushing her long hair. She looked at him in the mirror and licked her lips.

"Isn't it customary to knock?" she asked.

"Senna chastised me with her eyes for doin' the

115

same thing downstairs." He walked over, got a grip on her chin and twisted her mouth up to meet his. She cringed.

"I'm going to town and get the boy," he announced, tossing his hat on the bed and settling next to it.

"Don't you know that a hat on a bed is bad luck? Why are you bringing the boy out here?"

"It's only right that he be here when we're married." When he saw her white teeth clenched he smiled to himself.

"I see you're bound and determined to go through with it, Craig."

"We're in love."

She was wearing a wrapper which she drew tighter around her curves. The sight of her fired his blood but he would exercise his willpower. There were things to do first.

"Just thought I'd let you know about the boy. Have Senna clean out the sewing room so he can have his old quarters back."

Then he was gone. He rode to town with Joplin and Petey Sagar. Keeping to back streets, he reached the Adderly house.

There he exuded charm as he called for the boy. "Delira wants you out at the ranch. And so do I." He beamed down on Rance Borling who stood at Mike Adderly's side, looking defiant and a little scared.

"Where's Lassiter?" the boy wanted to know. "At Muleshoe?"

"Lassiter's gone to New Mexico. He asked me to tell you good-bye."

This news caused Rance's face to fall. "But why'd he go and not come by and say somethin'?"

Moran lowered what was meant to be a comforting hand to the boy's shoulder. Rance jerked away, which caused Moran's face to color. But he kept his voice level.

"Lassiter's a drifter, I thought you knew that. He's got a rep for it, Rance, so don't feel bad about it."

The Adderlys, husband and wife, stood stiffly in the small parlor with its horsehide sofa, with some of the stuffing coming out. The overweight Mrs. Adderly was wiping plump hands on an apron.

"You sure this is what Mrs. Borling wants?" she got up nerve enough to ask.

"She's the one sent me for the boy."

"Oh." She glanced at her husband who no doubt was silently waving farewell to the money Muleshoe had been paying for the boy's keep. A team and wagon rattled past the house and went on down the street, its driver singing loudly.

When Rance reluctantly said he had better get his things together, Moran thought quickly; he didn't want further delay. "Mrs. Borling bought you new clothes."

"But . . ."

"I'll send one of the men back to pick up your old things."

Finally, the ordeal was over after Moran was forced to shake Adderly's hand and then plant a kiss on his wife's fat cheek, which made her giggle like a schoolgirl.

Once outside, Moran wiped his lips on the back of his hand. They had a horse for the boy and Moran boosted him into the saddle where he sat hunched, looking forlorn. Sagar and Joplin remained silent, two lumpy shadows in the growing twilight. The first stars were beginning their nightly march across the heavens.

"Petey, you take charge of the boy," Moran ordered. "Rance, Petey's a good man." The boy said nothing.

They started off down the street, walking their horses, Moran giving Joplin a nod to fall back. A wind had come up, blowing loose ends of hair, zooming up pants legs.

"I'm gonna stay in town," Moran said softly. "Take the boy and lose him."

"Lose him? Whaddya mean?" Joplin turned his broad face that was marked from his encounter with Lassiter—the abrasions, the smashed nose.

"Take him somewhere far out where you think he won't be able to find his way back. Then say that Petey's horse came up with a loose shoe. And that when you stopped to examine it, the boy slipped away from you. You hunted all over hell for him, but lost him in the dark."

"Yeah, I see what you mean."

"You come in and tell me all this, then we'll all go looking for the kid. In the wrong direction, of course."

"Sure." Joplin's teeth showed faintly in the deepening shadows.

"By the time he's found, it'll be too late."

Moran rode up to where Petey Sagar and the boy were moving slowly. "Rance, I've got business in town. You go on with Petey and Joplin. I'll see you out at Muleshoe."

For effect, he gave the boy a friendly slap on the arm. But Rance, huddled in the saddle, just stared at him.

Does the damned kid sense what I'm up to? Moran wondered. Then in the next breath he told himself it was impossible. The kid still hadn't recovered from being abandoned by Lassiter, his so-called friend.

"See you boys at the ranch," Moran said heartily, turned his horse and loped in the direction of Trail's End.

There he poured himself a drink with steady hand and downed it. Getting rid of the boy was important. And it was wise to do it while Jim Sloan was away so there wouldn't be an inquisitive sheriff to wonder why it took so long to find the boy.

With Rance Borling out of the picture, Delira would have clear title to Muleshoe, free from the boy's share of the inheritance.

He had only a wisp of conscience when he faced the truth, that he was in reality murdering a seven-year-old boy. But it had to be done. He had always sensed that sometime in his life he would stumble upon good fortune. He'd almost had it in partnership with Dave Ashburn. But Dave had watched his chance and run. And before Moran finally tracked him down, Ashburn had gambled most of their money in high-stakes games. What he had left was put into the Hopeville livery stable.

But on the heels of that disaster loomed another even greater opportunity—a beautiful, hot-blooded widow who owned the biggest spread in this part of the territory.

Turning it over in his mind this way made him feel

better. He poured a second drink and engaged the saloon owner, Marcus Kane, in conversation. Kane's face was generously laced with small red veins, attesting to a fondness for his own whiskey.

"When're you an' Missus Borling gettin' hitched?" he wanted to know.

"Day after tomorrow," Moran said with a straight face. Of course, the boy would be missing and the nuptials postponed until he was found. By then, despite their grief over the boy being found dead, the ceremony would proceed.

"Reckon you can keep a tighter rein on her than Borling did," was the saloon owner's comment.

Just how much did Kane know, anyhow? Moran found himself wondering. Did he know about the late Dave Ashburn and Delira? And only the Lord knew how many others the lady had seduced with her wiles.

"She'll be a dutiful wife," Moran said and looked Kane in the eye.

"I expect she will, with you holdin' the reins," Kane responded nervously. "Have a drink on the house. From my special bottle." Kane, with pomaded graying hair, wearing a checkered vest, turned and with a gold key unlocked a small compartment in the back of the bar. He withdrew a bottle of Colonel's Choice.

"Fine whiskey, Moran. The best."

It's what I'll drink regularly, Moran wanted to say. Once Delira and I are man and wife.

# Chapter Twelve

Senna was singing under her breath as she prepared supper when the kitchen door opened. A boot scraped on the hardwood floor. She turned, blanched, then said shakily, "Lassiter. You gave me a start, you did."

A half-hour before, he had glimpsed Moran with Sagar and Joplin heading in the direction of town. Seeing Moran had activated a plan that had been simmering far back in his mind. Knowing he would have to move fast, he rode for Muleshoe at a gallop. He left his horse back in the trees and approached the two-story ranch house. Lamplight glowed in most of the downstairs windows but in only one window on the second floor.

Through one of the windows, Lassiter could see Senna moving heavily about the kitchen, tasting from a pot and stoking the fire in the big range. He had always gotten along with Senna. Timmie had told him that her late husband had been *segundo*, a job Lassiter had taken over before being falsely imprisoned for killing Dave Ashburn.

Loren Zane Grey

Senna quickly recovered from her fright and lowered her voice to a whisper when Lassiter put a finger across his lips.

"It's dangerous for you here, Lassiter. Moran . . ."

He told her Moran was on his way to town. "Tell me, Senna, how much of the old crew is left here at Muleshoe?"

She frowned, pursed her full lips, then said, "Reckon less than a dozen. Moran got rid of most the old-timers one by one when he took over." She stepped close and gripped Lassiter by the arms, looking up into his dark face. "What a relief that you're gonna help us. You are, ain't you?"

Lassiter nodded. "Where's Mrs. Borling?"

"Upstairs about to take a bath, she is." Senna made a disgruntled face. "I toted gallons of hot water upstairs, seems like."

"I want words with the lady."

Leaving the kitchen, Lassiter began to silently climb the stairs two at a time. He knocked on the door he remembered Timmie and his wife had shared.

"Come in, Senna, come in and make sure the water is hotter. What you brought is luke warm. . . ."

Delira's voice faded and her mouth slowly opened as she stared from the tub up at the tall, black-haired man in range clothes who stood with his back to her bedroom door.

"Lassiter," she breathed.

She sat very still in a zinc tub decorated on the sides with clusters of red roses, but the paint was beginning to fade. She was hunched so that only the upper parts

# GET
# 4 FREE BOOKS!

You can have the best Westerns delivered to your door for less than what you'd pay in a bookstore or online. Sign up for one of our book clubs today, and we'll send you **4 FREE\* BOOKS**, worth $23.96, just for trying it out...**with no obligation to buy, ever!**

---

Authors include classic writers such as
LOUIS L'AMOUR, MAX BRAND, ZANE GREY
and more; PLUS new authors such as
COTTON SMITH, TIM CHAMPLIN, JOHNNY D. BOGGS
and others.

---

As a book club member you also receive the following special benefits:
- **30% OFF** all orders through our website & telecenter!
- **Exclusive access** to special discounts!
- **Convenient** home delivery and 10 days to return any books you don't want to keep.

**There is no minimum number of books to buy,**
and you may cancel membership at any time.
See back to sign up!

\*Please include $2.00 for shipping and handling.

# YES!

Sign me up for the Leisure Western Book Club
and send my FOUR FREE BOOKS! If I choose to stay
in the club, I will pay only $13.44* each month,
a savings of $10.52!

NAME: _____

ADDRESS: _____

_____

TELEPHONE: _____

E-MAIL: _____

☐ I WANT TO PAY BY CREDIT CARD.

☐ VISA ☐ MasterCard ☐ DISCOVER

ACCOUNT #: _____

EXPIRATION DATE: _____

SIGNATURE: _____

Send this card along with $2.00 shipping & handling to:

**Leisure Western Book Club**
**20 Academy Street**
**Norwalk, CT 06850-4032**

Or fax (must include credit card information!) to: 610.995.9274.
You can also sign up online at www.dorchesterpub.com.

*Plus $2.00 for shipping. Offer open to residents of the U.S. and Canada only.
Canadian residents please call 1.800.481.9191 for pricing information.

If under 18, a parent or guardian must sign. Terms, prices and conditions subject to change. Subscription subject
to acceptance. Dorchester Publishing reserves the right to reject any order or cancel any subscription.

JOIN NOW!

of her breasts were visible. Steam from the bathwater made ringlets of dark red hair across her forehead, although she had piled most of it atop her head, held by a green ribbon. She was holding a jar of French soap that she had used to lather herself generously. It had made the bathwater murky and produced a froth of suds on the surface.

"What are you doing here, Lassiter?" she finally blurted. Then she laughed and with a display of mock modesty covered her breasts with her crossed arms. "Foolish to ask what you're doing here. Looking at me, you are, what else?"

Excitement flickered in her gray eyes and her mouth was open, her pink tongue delicately exploring her lower lip as she watched him.

"Moran's on his way to town. . . ."

"I know." She squirmed up straighter in the tub, no longer trying to hide herself. "You're planning something against him, aren't you?" she gasped, reaching out to clutch his wrist with her wet fingers. He had come to stand beside the tub. He handed her a large towel from the back of a chair.

"You told me you want to be rid of Moran."

"Yes, yes, *yes!*" Her teeth gleamed in the light of a cut-glass lamp on a dressing table.

"Will you face up to your crew? Fire the ones that Moran brought in and keep the old-timers?"

"Oh, my God, how perfect . . . how perfect!"

"Providing they want to stay and fight. Because Moran, if I know him, won't take this lying down."

"Of course he won't."

123

"Now's the time to make our move, while Moran's away."

"*Our* move. Oh, how I love the sound of that, Lassiter."

With that, she hopped out of the tub, being slow to drape herself in the towel.

"We'll have to move fast. I'll wait for you downstairs."

Her heart sang as she hastily dried, donned a camisole, then took a moment to run a comb through her long damp hair. How perfectly things were working out for her. In time she might even marry him when she decided to settle down at last. . . .

In front of the Muleshoe bunkhouse, Lassiter called out, "Mrs. Borling's coming in. You men make yourselves decent."

He waited a few moments, then looked in. Several of the cowhands were grabbing pants and shirts. When the crew saw Lassiter, they grew silent and exchanged glances in the lamplight.

"Howdy, Lassiter," a few of them said. "Glad to see you back here."

The face of five riders, however, tightened and their eyes grew wary. These were men Lassiter didn't know. The others had been working for Timmie Borling when Lassiter had come on as *segundo*.

"All right, Mrs. Borling," Lassiter said, holding the door for her.

She walked in regally, her chin lifted, and nodded imperiously to some of the men.

"I'm taking over temporarily as foreman," Lassiter announced. "Craig Moran no longer draws pay here."

At this news, Delira first look surprised, then pleased. Some of the tension went out of her shoulders.

"Am I right, Mrs. Borling?" Lassiter asked crisply, turning to the lady.

"It is what I want," she responded happily.

Lassiter put his attention on the five newcomers that Moran had hired on after Borling and Lassiter were sent to prison. "Are these men fired, Mrs. Borling?"

"They are," she announced.

"Hey, wait a minute," a black-bearded man named Sam Dirk snarled. "We was hired on by Craig Moran an' we don't move till he gives the word."

"You better get an ear horn, my friend," Lassiter said coldly, "because I said Moran isn't working here any longer. You five get your gear together and clear out."

The five men looked at each other. Then Dirk shrugged, and started to roll up his blankets. Suddenly, with his hairy black hand, he reached for a gun rig hanging from a nail on his bunk.

Before he could touch the weapon, however, Lassiter's .44 was leveled and cocked.

Sam Dirk came up short, he eyes widened at the speed of Lassiter's draw.

Lassiter turned to the other nine men. "You boys worked for me before. Do you want to again, or do you want your time?"

To a man they wanted to stay on at Muleshoe.

Despite much grumbling from Sam Dirk and his four cohorts, Lassiter ordered their weapons threaded on a catch rope through the trigger guards.

"You can pick 'em up a the Hopeville livery barn."

"When?" Dirk snarled.

"Maybe next week. Maybe the week after."

"Pretty damn smart, ain't you?" Dirk's teeth showed through his black beard.

"I just figure to avoid trouble as long as possible," Lassiter stated in a flat voice.

When the weapons were collected, the warbags of the five were searched for extra guns. Only one was found, a two-shot derringer belonging to Sam Dirk. He grumbled more at the loss of the small weapon than he did at confiscation of his .45 and Winchester.

"You boys know the boundaries of Muleshoe," Lassiter said, looking each man in the eye in turn. "Stay on the far side of the line. Trespassers will be shot."

Delira went back to the house, her gray eyes lively, a smile on her lips.

When the sullen five men had saddled up and were ready to ride out, Lassiter gave them a final warning.

"Stay off Muleshoe."

Knowing Moran wouldn't take this lightly, Lassiter set out guards. He would take his own turn after midnight.

"We've got to save something for Timmie Borling's son," Lassiter said to the nine who were left on the Muleshoe payroll. "The only way to do that is to have cows to sell. We'll start roundup in three days."

Ellen Stencoe bit the end of a pen in the hotel room that Lassiter had suggested she take, and stared at the faded yellow wallpaper while she tried to compose a letter in her head. At last, she dipped a pen point into a jar of ink she had borrowed from the hotel desk and began to write.

*Dear Ralph,*

*What I am about to tell you may hurt you, which I certainly don't mean to do, my dear. But I might as well come directly to the point. While here, I've met the most wonderful man. His name is Lassiter and I'm sure you'd like each other if you could ever bring yourself to forgive me. What I am trying to say, dear Ralph, is that I intend to marry this man. I expect we'll do considerable traveling because I've heard that he doesn't like to stay too long in one place. One day we might even get down to Tucson. I would love to see you again, Ralph, because I have only fond memories for what we've meant to each other.*

*Please, please say that we can be friends, because to be enemies would crush my heart. Do wish the best for me as I do for you. Keep looking and you'll find someone more suited to you than Ellen Stencoe. You could do worse than pick Diana Cramer. I know she worships you—she always has. I must close now and mail this because I expect to see Lassiter shortly.*

*Fondly,*
*Your friend, Ellen*

Tears welled up in her eyes despite her resolve to remain calm. After addressing the envelope, she took the letter out to the desk and dropped it in the mail slot.

Returning to her room, she put on a dress she had bought that afternoon at the Mercantile. It was white with small blue flowers. She was sure that Lassiter would agree that it made her look quite fetching.

When Lassiter didn't come within the hour, she left a note for him and started for a cafe across from the Trail's End. The hotel served only one day a week, Sunday dinner, she had learned.

As she was crossing the street, the wind whipping at her skirts, she had to bend down to control them. A man laughed, softly, pleasantly. Turning, she saw Craig Moran just stepping from the saloon.

He hurried to her, saying, "A lady's dress balloons on such an evening."

She made no comment, and continued on her way. But he caught up, gripped her by an arm, bringing her to a halt. An odor of whiskey was on his breath. He looked down at her, his hazel eyes filled with amusement.

"Turn me loose, if you don't mind," she snapped, and tried to free herself. But his grip was too tight.

"Why don't you let me buy you supper? And afterwards . . . Muleshoe has quarters at the hotel. You'll have plenty of room to spread out." He was chuckling, obviously fairly drunk.

"A revolting suggestion," she said in the hardest voice she could manage.

It caused his face to change so abruptly that it produced a cold fear uncoiling along her spine.

"Don't get uppity with me," he said, his voice beginning to thicken. "My men said you spent the night with Lassiter out at your brother's shack."

"Your men," she said scathingly before she could

catch herself, "that you sent to commit murder."

"Not at all. Only to talk, but Lassiter decided to shoot instead."

Jerking her arm so hard she almost fell, she managed to free herself and hurry on across the street.

Just before entering the cafe, she looked back and saw him standing unsteadily in the center of the rutted street, glaring after her.

With a thudding heart she sat at a table and looked at the menu. It was dirty and stained. She halfway expected Moran to come storming in and try to drag her to the Muleshoe suite. But he didn't come. She forced herself to eat, although the food was dry and tasteless. A small child was crying at a nearby table and a woman wearing a sun bonnet was arguing with a man. Probably her husband. And at the same time she was trying to shush the child.

When Ellen returned to the hotel, she entered by the rear door and crept to her room. Her note for Lassiter was still stuck in the door. Letting herself in, she dragged a chair over to the door and put its back under the knob. Then she sat down on the bed to wait for Lassiter.

While far out in the mountains, a young boy was being led deeper and deeper into the wilds. . . .

# Chapter Thirteen

Rance Borling was cold and getting scared. He eyed the two big shadowed figures that flanked him, riding so close that at times their legs brushed his.

"This ain't the way to Muleshoe," he said tremulously for the third time.

"We're taking the long way," Joplin said at last, which brought a dry laugh from Petey Sagar.

Somehow the laugh was more frightening than the long silence during the ride out of town. By now black clouds had drifted in to cover the moon and in patches of sky stars were barely visible as if seen through gauze. A breeze had come up, bringing with it the smell of creosote and pine needles. The wind bit through Rance's light coat and into his spine and shoulders.

"Where're you takin' me?" he asked at last after a long climb up a steep slope.

"We'll be there soon," Joplin grunted.

"I don't think so. You're not takin' me home, you're . . ."

"Keep your mouth shut, kid," Petey Sagar snarled.

From his open mouth floated a blast of whiskey fumes. Rance realized that every time Sagar had dropped back, he took a pull at a bottle. At the top of the grade they halted to let the horses blow. Here white stars blazed from a clearing sky. With the horses snorting and stomping, from the ground came a hum of insects. Rance brushed them away from his face, which was coated with sweat despite the chill wind blowing from higher peaks.

"This is far enough," Sagar snapped after a minute or so.

"We'll go down the far side a few miles," said Joplin, standing up in the stirrups to peer ahead.

"Down there ain't the way to Muleshoe!" Rance cried. "I know it isn't! What are you two tryin' to *do!*"

Before either man could answer, he drubbed his horse's flanks with his heels, reined it in a tight circle and started away at a gallop. It was a quarter of a mile down a dangerous shale-strewn slope, with the two men pounding along behind, before they caught him.

"You little bastard," Sagar yelled. "We coulda busted our necks chasin' you!"

Joplin reached over and seized the reins of Rance's horse. "You set that saddle, sonny, or I'll give you a quirtin'."

They led him back to the summit and far down the other side, a land of immense rocks that loomed ghostly in the darkness. Faint moonlight etched high canyon walls.

"This is it," Joplin finally announced, and pulled Rance from the saddle and set him not too gently down on the ground. "Come on, Petey, let's get outta here. I hope you saved some of that bottle for me. I can use a drink."

Rance cried out and tried to run blindly after them, but they led his horse away at a fast clip. Soon the towering rocks and shadows swallowed them up. Panting, he finally halted and leaned against a pine, listening to the fading sound of hoofs beating against the night.

At last there was silence and he was alone with only the sounds of wild things. Tears pushed at his eyes and his mouth trembled. Then he thought of his father, knowing he would want him to be a man.

He had no idea where he was. All he could do was try to backtrack the way they had come into this wild stretch of country. . . .

Moran, with one foot hooked over the brass rail in the Trail's End, brooded about the lovely woman who early that night had dismissed him like he was some two-bit cowhand. The more he drank, the deeper it bit into him. He had halfway decided to break into her hotel room, and put a hand over her mouth when Sam Dirk and four other Muleshoe men entered the saloon.

Moran scowled, not liking the looks on their faces. Sam Dirk came right to the point.

*"Lassiter!"* Moran swore and banged his glass on the bar with such force that it shattered. Other drinkers turned to stare with apprehension at his livid face.

Instantly, he was stone sober, his busy mind already planning a countermove. He pushed the bottle down the bar to his men.

"Help yourselves," he grunted, then put his mind back on the problem at hand.

\* \* \*

It was long past midnight when Joplin and Sagar, both of them fairly drunk, approached Muleshoe headquarters. Miles back they had turned the boy's horse loose where it was bound to be found by searchers.

Inside the Muleshoe line they were challenged by two night guards, one of them Lassiter. Both men looked surprised. Under the menace of cocked rifles, the grumbling pair were disarmed.

Joplin had a final word as they started along the town road. "Lassiter, have you got a surprise comin' to you!" he shouted, meaning the boy.

Lassiter thought of calling him back to demand what the surprise could be. Then he decided it was just boasting, and let him go.

The next morning Lassiter intended to send out word from the Mercantile in town that it was payday for the cowhands who had been fired. He would take four men with him. He had already figured out what each discharged rider had coming. Delira had wisely kept the combination to the ranch safe, not letting Moran get his hands on it.

As he counted out the gold pieces, her hand brushed his; there was invitation in her eyes. But he told her bluntly that he had the boy on his mind that early morning.

And after Lassiter had gone, Delira also had the boy on her mind. Moran had said he was bringing the boy. Where was he? Had something happened? Then she shrugged and decided not to burden herself with the problem.

\* \* \*

In town, from the front window of the Mercantile, Lassiter watched children heading for school, but no Rance. Perhaps the boy had slipped past him while he was paying off one of the grumbling cowhands.

At last the job was done. Lassiter thanked Silas Rimmley for the use of the store. He was heading for the door when Moran entered, wearing a stiff smile.

"You kinda took over out at Muleshoe, it seems," he said softly.

"For Rance Borling is why I did it."

Moran laughed. "You're too big for your britches, Lassiter, way too big."

Other customers in the store stiffened and some of them edged for the side door that opened onto a loading platform. Silas Rimmley's eyes grew round behind his steel-framed glasses.

"I don't want no trouble in here," he said nervously.

This drew another laugh from Moran, but his hazel eyes were ugly as he turned on Lassiter. "You're not gonna get away with this," he warned, his lips drawn over his teeth in a hard grin. "But I s'pose you can figure that out already."

Lassiter didn't bother to reply, but led his four men out the side door. They thumped down the steps of the loading platform to a vacant lot.

"What now, Lassiter?" asked a lank man named Bob Ellick.

"I'm going to collect the boy. Then we'll go back to the ranch. Watch your drinking."

Lassiter rode down to the school, tied his horse and entered the building, hat in hand. A Miss Adams was teaching a class of youngsters about Rance's age. He asked for the boy.

"He didn't come to school today," she said sharply, remembering that he was one of those who had been part of the uproar the night of the school dance.

Following her mention of the incident, Lassiter didn't accept her word about the boy. Another teacher was asked with the same result. Rance Borling hadn't come to school that day.

Faintly worried, Lassiter rode by side streets to the Adderly house. Lassiter crossed a weed-choked front yard to knock on the door. Adderly wasn't around, but his wife was. When he asked for Rance, the sullen look deepened on her plump face.

"Took him away, he did."

"Who're you talking about?"

"Craig Moran. He came for the boy."

Cold knifed through Lassiter as if someone had thrust open a door on a frigid morning. "Moran took Rance away?"

"Took him to Muleshoe, I reckon. Looks like we won't git no more money for the boy's keep."

"Are you lying to me, Mrs. Adderly?"

"I sure ain't an' you got no right to think I am." Her double chins wobbled in agitation.

Lassiter insisted on searching the house. In the boy's room he found clothing but no Rance.

Then he searched the town for Moran, but failed to find him.

He did run into Ellen Stencoe in front of the hotel, looking fresh and pretty. But Lassiter's mood made it impossible for him to pay much attention to her. When he told her about the boy, her blue eyes darkened with concern. This morning she wore a green dress and her dark hair was piled atop her shapely head.

When he told her he'd be staying out at Muleshoe for a while, she looked faintly worried. Then she managed a warm smile.

"I'm here waiting, my dear," she assured him, gripped his hand and looked meaningfully up into his eyes.

If Lassiter hadn't already been preoccupied with Rance, her attitude might have been troubling to him.

Before parting, she said that Moran undoubtedly had taken Rance to the ranch, then returned to town. Lassiter frowned. It was possible, he conceded. "But this morning Mrs. Borling didn't mention Rance at all. Unless she thought it unimportant."

"Where did you sleep last night?"

"In the bunkhouse. Why?"

"Oh, just thinking of you and . . . and Mrs. Borling."

"Well, don't," he snapped in a colder voice than intended.

"I could very well be jealous," Ellen said, trying to smile. But her teeth were nibbling on her lower lip and there was worry in her eyes.

Lassiter barely heard her, however. He was anxious to get out to Muleshoe and see if Rance was there.

Lifting a hand, he whirled and went to his horse. He and his four men rode quickly out of town in the direction of Muleshoe. He didn't look around to note the sudden hurt reflected on Ellen's face, nor the way she disconsolately walked into the hotel.

All of his energy was focused on the boy; time enough to brace himself for the coming battle with Moran.

The ride to Muleshoe seemed endless. The two guards Lassiter had stationed at the main entrance to the ranch raised their rifles to acknowledge their presence. Lassiter pulled up. One of the men was Chuck Bradford, lean and slightly stooped. His vest was a faded red color. Lassiter asked him if he'd seen the boy.

"Nary hide nor hair, Lassiter. He's in town, ain't he?"

Lassiter shook his head and told the men to keep their eyes open. At the main house he met Senna, whose lumpy face grew worried when he asked her about Rance.

"But he ain't here, Lassiter."

"He's got to be."

He went bounding up the stairs. This time, Delira was in her bedroom fully clothed. Only for an instant did she seem annoyed at the way he burst in, his narrowed eyes sweeping her room. Then her lips parted and she stepped toward him, her hands outstretched. But he didn't take them. He asked about the boy. She shook her head.

Quickly, he told her of the scene with Mrs. Adderly. "If Rance isn't here, it means Moran's got him," he said angrily.

"Just be careful, Lassiter. It's all I ask."

The four men he had taken to town were about to ride out, to start moving cattle for the roundup. He called them in and told them about the boy. Their faces hardened at the grim news.

Since learning about the boy from Mrs. Adderly, Lassiter had gone under the assumption that Moran wouldn't *dare* bring harm to the boy. Public opinion would be too great against him. But he was wrong.

# Chapter Fourteen

It had been a night of terror for Rance Borling. After being abandoned by Joplin and Sagar, he had hiked for miles in what he hoped was the right direction that would take him to Muleshoe. Just before dawn he crested a long grade where shadows were deep under a giant ridge of overhanging rocks. Wind cut through his flimsy jacket and his clothing. A moon sailed now in a cloudless sky, which was some comfort. But he saw not one familiar landmark as he looked around.

One time his father had taken him on roundup for a couple of days and at night had made a game out of trying to teach him the stars. But by now Rance's mind was so confused due to his increasing fright that he couldn't remember how to locate the North Star. And even if he did find it, what good would it do? He didn't know whether Muleshoe was east or west. Or north or south, for that matter.

At last, he huddled in exhaustion, sheltered from the wind in a cleft of rocks. His mind ceased its senseless gyrations and settled down so he could think logically.

It was obvious that Joplin and Sagar had deliberately gotten him lost; with one ending in mind—that he would stay lost and eventually die out here in the wilderness.

Facing the reality of his situation made his mouth start to tremble. But he stiffened his lips, vowing not to give way. Just thinking of his father a few minutes before had brought a sting into his eyes. Now he felt a warm tear slide down his cheek and into a corner of his mouth. It tasted salty.

He was suddenly aware of a rank smell and a soft, padding sound. Sitting up in alarm, he looked around. Gradually his eyes adjusted to the deeper shadows not quite reached by a fringe of moonlight. One of the shadows was moving toward him, emitting small growling noises.

Instinctively, he knew what it was and his heart thumped coldly in his chest. A bear. Because of the darkness he couldn't tell whether it was black or brown. That it was alive was enough for him.

In panic, he scrambled straight up the tilted rocks where he had sought shelter. In the open the wind was strong and biting. His sudden movement brought a louder growl from the bear and it began to come up the granite incline after him. On all fours, Rance looked back, his heart pounding, and saw the bear close enough to take a swipe at his right foot. It missed. But the mighty swing of the paw threw the animal off balance. It emitted a mighty roar and began to slowly slide back down the steep rock slant until its claws again found purchase in soil.

Rance knew it would be after him again. Desperately, he scrambled on up the slope where he clung to a huge bald rock and looked around. He was at the high point of the ridge, and beyond a clearing of some thirty yards was a great bank of dark trees.

He could hear the bear's claws scraping the stone ascent, still uttering low growls. All Rance could think about was possible safety in the trees.

He burst over the top of the bald rock and ran wildly down the other side, his breath whistling, as fast as he could go. Sweat stung his eyes and it seemed that his heart would explode. As the first of the trees loomed up, he chose one with a thick limb over six feet from the ground. Above it more limbs jutted into the darkness.

Not breaking his frantic stride, he launched himself through the air, praying that he had judged the distance correctly, his hands outstretched. In the great zooming arc, his fingertips brushed the tree limb. He turned cold, believing he had missed. But his open hands closed solidly over the limb. His palms were scraped by bark and a shower of it came down onto his hair. But momentum swung him up and over so that he straddled the limb.

Already he could see the bear coming across the clearing at an ambling run. Frantically, Rance began to climb higher into the tree as the bear emitted growls of frustration. It slapped the tree, shaking it so hard that Rance's heart jammed his throat.

Then he saw the apparent reason for the bear's displeasure. Ambling down the slope in the moonlight came two cubs. Evidently, he had taken shelter near a bear's cave and the animal had thought he was in some way a threat to her offspring.

Several times the bear slapped the tree, bringing

down a shower of leaves while the cubs milled about at her feet.

After nearly an hour of circling the tree, its nose in the air, growling intermittently, it at last started up the mountain, the two cubs racing to keep up. But even after he lost sight of the bear, Rance stayed in the tree. He was taking no chances.

Several times he dozed off, catching himself just before he crashed to the ground. Each time it gave him such a start that he would stay awake for a time without slipping into sleep.

Then he saw a rim of faint light to the east. Huddled on the tree limb, his back to the trunk, he watched the sun slowly climb the world to start a new day.

From time to time he peered through the thick tree branches for any sign of the bear. But he saw nothing. Had the bear given up on him? Or was it lying in wait? His stomach rumbled, but he had no way to get food. He had no gun, just his bare hands.

Finally, in desperation, he lowered himself and dropped from the first limb to the ground. It was quite a drop and it jarred his heels. It was a miracle he had ever been able to leap high enough to grab the limb.

Cautiously, he walked deeper into the trees, casting a glance over his shoulder at every other step. But still there was no sign of the bear. A great sigh of relief escaped him.

All he found to eat were a few wild strawberries. Never had anything tasted as good. He walked and walked, the sun at his back, until reaching another ridge. After a long climb, scraping his knees, bruising his hands, he reached the top. While taking a few moments to get his breath, he stood up and looked around, hoping desperately for some landmark, a smudge of smoke or Pride's Point, which projected from the earth like a giant thumb. Shading his eyes, he studied all four points of the compass. But he saw nothing. Trying not to take on the added burden of despair, he was determined to be cheerful.

But soon the wall he had built against his emotions began to totter and finally crumble. That was when he slumped to the ground, put his head on his knees and wept in his fear and frustration. He was lost, completely lost with no idea in which direction lay Muleshoe or Hopeville. All he could see from the vantage point were miles of forested canyons and towering red rock walls. Overhead a hawk soared and Rance thought, If I could only get up as high as you I could probably see Muleshoe.

Lassiter returned to town with his four men. At the Trail's End, no one had seen Moran since the night before. He crossed to the hotel, with the four men hurrying to catch up.

T. C. Jones, who owned the hotel, a plump bald man with a thick mustache, swore that Moran wasn't occupying the Muleshoe suite. But Lassiter demanded to have a look. With a sigh, Jones climbed the stairs and opened the door of the suite with his spare key.

But there was no sign of Moran in the two rooms. One was fitted out as a parlor, the other a bedroom. Lassiter had stayed over here several nights with Timmie Borling when the latter was too drunk to set a saddle.

"Why're you in such a sweat to see Moran, any-how?" Jones wanted to, know.

"It looks like he's kidnapped Rance Borling."

"The hell you say." Jones's jaw dropped.

"Why'd that damn sheriff pick a time like this to go up to the capital?" Lassiter complained, banging his fist against the wall.

"Sloan said he wouldn't be gone more'n a week or so," Jones put in. "First time he's never named a deputy when he figured to be away for a spell."

"The bastard likely wanted the place to erupt while he was gone. Then when he came back he'd put the pieces back together."

Jones stared at him, but Lassiter was already slamming his way down the narrow stairway.

He found Ellen Stencoe waiting for him.

"I saw you come in," she said hopefully, then bit her lip at sight of the men with him. "Lassiter, is something the matter?" The men went outside.

When Lassiter told her what had happened she whitened. "How awful," she whispered. "Should I go out to Muleshoe and keep Mrs. Borling company? Do you think she'd like that?"

Lassiter shook his head. "Stay away from Muleshoe." Then he patted her arm to show that he didn't mean it like it sounded. But nevertheless there was hurt in her eyes.

He was upset, not thinking straight. He'd had only a few hours of sleep. Most of the night he had ridden in circles, trying to locate Moran. Shortly after dawn he had started out for town again.

"When can I expect you back, Lassiter?" Ellen Stencoe asked softly, but he was already hurrying away.

He found Mike Adderly just leaving his house. Now that he and his wife no longer would receive payment for taking care of the boy, he was going back to his old job as hostler at the livery barn. At sight of Lassiter's dark angry face, he grew wary and stepped back into the house.

"What you want?" he asked in a quavering voice.

"I want you to think back to when Moran came and took the boy. Did he say where he was going to take him?"

"Never a word about that." Mrs. Adderly was peering fearfully into the room.

Lassiter argued with her husband, saying the man must have remembered *something*. That was when his wife mentioned the two men who had accompanied Moran.

"Moran turned the kid right over to them an' then he rode back downtown, like he was goin' to the Trail's End."

"What two men?"

"One of 'em was the big fella you first fought with that day at the wagon yard," she said.

"Joplin," Lassiter said angrily. "Who was the other one?"

"He works for Muleshoe, him an' his brother." She described the man at Lassiter's insistence. Petey Sagar. A fine pair to kidnap a boy. And what else was it but that?

144

Mike Adderly turned on his wife. "Whyn't you tell me, woman? So I could be the one to let Lassiter know. . . ."

But Lassiter fled the scene of the domestic argument.

He was enraged at himself for not having gotten the information the night before. He told his four men to scour the town for sign of either one of the pair.

But it was Lassiter who located Petey Sagar. The man was riding into the livery barn, whistling under his breath.

When Lassiter stepped from behind one of the stalls, his face fell and he made a desperate grab for his gun. But Lassiter leaped, got him by a foot and pulled him from the saddle. He struck the hay-littered runway hard.

"My leg!" he cried and rubbed his thigh which had been slashed by Lassiter's bullet down at the Crossroads.

"Where's Joplin?" Lassiter demanded.

Sagar's eyes were suddenly crafty. "Don't rightly know."

Lassiter disarmed him, then said, "It won't matter a damn bit. I've got you. And that's all I need."

After throwing Sagar's revolver and rifle into a hay mow, he ordered the man back into the saddle. Then the two of them rode out of the livery barn. Down the block, Lassiter saw Ellick and hailed him. It took only a few minutes to round up the other three men. Then they were all riding out of town, with Sagar in the middle.

After a mile, Lassiter demanded suddenly, "Where's the boy?"

"Don't know what you're talkin' about." Sagar had regained confidence after getting over his initial fright at meeting Lassiter in the livery barn.

"I'm not going to fool with you, Sagar," Lassiter said ominously.

"A lot of folks seen you ride me outta town. Anything happen to me an' you'll swing."

Lassiter drew rein at the edge of a clump of trees. "Ellick, make me a fire."

Sagar was pulled from the saddle as Ellick and the others hastily gathered brush and pine cones. Ellick got a fire going after using a pocketful of matches.

Sagar watched the growing fire nervously and paled when Lassiter ordered him to pull off his boots and socks.

"What . . . what you aim to do, anyhow?" Sagar faltered.

"Put your feet in the fire. Till you tell me what you did with the boy."

"Moran took him. I dunno what he done with him."

"He don't hear worth a damn," Lassiter said. "Ellick, you boys take off his boots and socks."

Two of them held a squirming Sagar by the arms and the third man held his legs. When Sagar's feet were bare, Lassiter dragged him over to the fire.

"Your last chance, Sagar."

"You can't get away with this. The sheriff'll . . ."

That was as far as he got. Sagar was sitting on the ground, his bare feet in a patch of sunlight. Seizing one of his legs, Lassiter hauled him down a gentle slope to the fire and brushed one of Sagar's feet past the flames.

A howl burst from Sagar. And when Lassiter looked

as if he intended to thrust the bare foot deeper into the flames, Sagar broke.

"I . . . I'll tell you. Only don't burn me. I go loco when I get near fire. My old man burned up in our barn . . . when I was just a kid. . . ."

After nearly an hour of riding, Sagar called a halt. "Near as I kin tell, we went up here." Sagar was pointing upgrade.

"You better damn well remember," was Lassiter's threat.

"Yeah, this is it." Sagar's voice still shook. He had not yet fully recovered from his bad scare.

As they climbed, dipped, going farther and farther away from Muleshoe, Lassiter had to restrain himself to keep from smashing Petey Sagar in the face. To bring a boy Rance's age all the way out in this wild country and then abandon him was unthinkable. Lassiter told Sagar as much as their horses plodded upward, slipping on shale, dust pluming in their wake.

"Wasn't me who done it, Lassiter," Sagar whined. "Joplin, he's the one."

"I'll deal with him later."

"He's a bastard, all right."

"Deal with him after I finish with you." Lassiter shot him a cold glance.

Sagar winced, as if Lassiter had struck him.

It took two tries before Sagar finally pinpointed the exact spot where they had left Rance. It was in the center of a vast canyon, surrounded by red rock crags, some of them leaning at what looked to be precarious angles. A warming sun appeared suddenly from a cloud bank.

One of the other men, Josh Billings, pointed at tracks made by a small pair of boots. "Looks like he went that way," and jabbed a thumb toward a high ridge to the west.

Lassiter had already seen the tracks, shuddering at the sight of them. For all he knew it might be the last tangible memory he'd have of the boy in all this wilderness.

They dodged around shed-sized rocks, the climb ever steepening. Finally, upon reaching the ridge, they let their horses blow.

In a few moments they heard a low growl in the distance. As they stared, a large brown bear emerged from a cave, with two cubs at her heels. When she reared up on hind legs, letting out a roar, Ellick raised his rifle. But Lassiter quickly pulled down the barrel and shook his head.

"We'll only shoot if it looks like she's going to make a try for us."

"She looks meaner'n hell." Ellick shivered as the bear roared again.

Then she wheeled abruptly and ambled off to the east, the cubs bouncing along at her heels. Just before entering a thick stand of pines, she looked around, uttered one last snarl and disappeared.

"I hope to hell the boy didn't come up against *that*," Lassiter said with a shake of his head. His cold eyes settled again on a cringing Sagar.

"Wasn't me who left the boy," he said in a thin, frightened voice. "I keep tellin' you that."

After resting the horses, they again picked up the boy's trail and pressed on.

It was then that Lassiter distinctly heard a rasping sound as if made by a shod hoof sliding on rock. There was instant silence. The sound had come from behind him. Here they were riding single file toward a great cluster of giant rocks.

Lassiter whipped around in the saddle and peered back up the brushy slope they had just descended.

"Watch it!" he cautioned.

For Blanchard, it was too late. One minute he was upright in the saddle and the next part of his face had disintegrated. His legs were jerking spasmodically as he fell to the ground. Ellick made a grab for the reins of the horse that was beginning to rear, but missed. The sound of a rifle ripped the stillness an instant later.

Far upslope was a twitching of brush, a puff of smoke that Lassiter spotted. His first shot was evidently wide of the target, but the second, to the left of where he had seen movement and the powdersmoke, brought a man staggering from cover. His arms were spread from his thick body and a rifle was beginning to slip from his right hand. In the center of the man's shirt a redness was already spreading. A lean-faced man, he plunged down with such force that his legs came up behind him, then settled to the ground. It was one of the Muleshoe riders Lassiter had fired, but he didn't know the man's name.

"Barney Korg," Ellick supplied as they spun their horses into the shelter of towering rocks as more rifles opened up.

"Spread out!" Lassiter shouted. "So we'll make a small target!"

As they were ordered, the men took up positions along the line of rocks, a good dozen feet between each man.

To Lassiter, the presence of the Muleshoe riders meant that Craig Moran was probably along. Also Joplin. As the names crossed his mind he turned cold. Joplin, who had murdered Rance's father; then had done his damnedest to let the son die from exposure or predators. Lassiter's hands grew slick on the rifle. . . .

Some miles to the west, Rance was wearily climbing an escarpment when he lost his balance. He fell hard, his right foot catching in a crevice. Blinding pain smashed through the boy. As he lay, cold sweat bathing his body, he saw a piece of shattered bone sticking from his leg. He fainted.

# Chapter Fifteen

Ducking low, Lassiter crept back to where Blanchard had fallen to try and detect signs of life. There were none. He hadn't expected any, really, because of the nature of his wound. Lassiter swore under his breath, knowing that every minute they were delayed in resuming their search for the boy increased his peril. Lifting his head, Lassiter saw nothing but open country beyond the rocks, which they would be forced to cross if they made a break from the sanctuary of their natural fortress.

By now the firing from above was sporadic, bullets occasionally whipping through the brush or ricocheting off one of the giant boulders.

Keeping down, Lassiter dragged Blanchard's body behind one of the rocks. He glanced at Sagar huddled nearby, noting an incipient look of triumph on his narrow face. Obviously, he was counting on Moran and the others to rescue him.

But Sagar caught Lassiter staring at him and the look vanished. Why couldn't it have been Sagar shot down instead of Blanchard? Lassiter wondered grimly.

A quick study of their situation convinced Lassiter that they could be pinned down here for the rest of the day. Meanwhile, the boy's danger increased by the hour.

Creeping to where Ellick was crouched, he outlined a plan. "If you think you can hold 'em off, I'll go on ahead. I'm worried about the boy. Moran might sneak down the other side, swing around and pick up Rance's tracks again."

"Yeah, you're right."

"That'd put him ahead of us and too close to wherever the boy might be."

"We'll hold 'em," Ellick said through clenched teeth. "Blanchard was my friend." He looked sourly at the crumpled figure on the ground. "I sure ain't forgettin' that."

Blanchard's horse had drifted off and was now placidly cropping grass some two hundred yards away in the brush at the base of a sheer wall of reddish stone.

Rifle in hand, Lassiter mounted up, the protecting rock higher than he was in the saddle. Billings and Crombie, the other two men, looked around, with concern on their brown faces.

"It's gonna be risky tryin' to bust outta these rocks," Joe Crombie said through a tangle of reddish beard.

Lassiter shrugged. "If Sagar tries to make a break, shoot him."

Then, bent low in the saddle, he took a deep breath and suddenly rammed in the spurs. The horse he had chosen at Muleshoe was a long-legged sorrel. It leaped from the protecting flange of rock, roaring across open space. There was a faint shout from above. A rifle opened up, then another and another. With answering fire from his own men.

Lassiter held on tensely, his cheek against the neck of the speeding horse. Bullets clipped brush and puckered the bare ground ahead of him. Just when he thought he was going to make it, he felt a shudder run through the horse and knew it had been hit.

Already he was looking for a place to land when its forelegs buckled and it came down hard, nose to the ground. There was a distinct snapping sound that reminded Lassiter of a tree limb breaking.

Deep in the brush, Lassiter struck the ground and rolled to take up some of the impact. Somehow he kept a grip on his rifle.

Instantly, he began moving at a crouching run through the brush in the direction of the cliff where he had last seen Blanchard's horse. Bullets began to seek him out, chewing up brush and whistling past his ears. But he kept up a zigzagging run to throw off the riflemen above. By now the range was long and getting longer.

The faint crackle of rifle fire and the sounds of Lassiter's approach caused Blanchard's roan to throw up its head.

"Hold it, boy!" Lassiter prayed as the distance between man and horse began to narrow. Taking a chance, he straightened up so as to make the last few yards at a dead run.

He saw the roan wheel, the eyes wide now. And it was then that Lassiter lunged and managed to get one hand on the reins that were looped against the saddle horn. In the same movement his left foot shot into a stirrup and the sudden spurt of the frightened horse shot him into the saddle. Bent low, he went pounding down the slope. He thought he heard faint cheering from Ellick and the others, but he couldn't be sure.

"I beat the bastards," he said through his teeth when he finally drew rein and began to study the ground for any sign of Rance. Soon he picked up the boy's trail again. Keeping his eyes open in case Moran had slipped away from his men and got ahead of him, he began to follow the signs Rance had left. A very tired kid, Lassiter realized, from the staggered set of boot prints.

It was late afternoon before he finally came upon the boy. The first thing Lassiter saw was the ugly break in the boy's leg. The sight of it turned him cold. The boy lay in a pocket of a sloping cliff that rose behind him into the azure sky. Some spruce and aspen had gained a foothold in the rocks.

Something caused the boy's eyelids to flutter and they flew open. One small hand closed over a rock he had evidently picked up to use as a weapon.

Upon recognizing Lassiter, he gave a glad cry that ended in a groan when he tried to sit up.

Lassiter was out of the saddle, kneeling beside the boy. "You'll be all right now, Rance," he said, trying to keep anger and despair from coloring his voice.

The boy looked emaciated, his eyes red from lack of sleep. For years, whenever on the trail, Lassiter had carried pemmican, whenever he could get his hands on any. A superior food of the traveling Indian, he had learned in his youth.

Cradling the boy in his arms, he fed him a little from a pouch. When Rance asked for more, Lassiter shook his head.

"A little at a time, Rance. Let's clear out of here. But first I've got to tend to you."

He sounded almost jovial as if splinting a broken leg was no great chore. But inwardly he was seething because he blamed Moran, Joplin and Sagar for the boy's condition. And they would pay dearly, he vowed.

At Muleshoe, Delira paced the parlor, kicking at the hem of her white dress each time she made a turn in the room. Her face was set, her lips pale. Lassiter had been gone for hours. And now Craig Moran was here, having bluffed his way past the guards Lassiter had set out.

When Delira accused him of doing something to Rance, he denied her accusation. "Hell, I wouldn't hurt the kid."

"Lassiter's gone to hunt for him," she said in her nastiest voice. "To undo what you've done."

"I know Lassiter's trying to find him. But I deny, as I said before, that I had anything to do with his disappearance."

"Why did you come out here, Craig? You were ordered to stay away."

This brought a smile to his handsome face and he rubbed at the nose that had once been broken and healed slightly crooked. "It shows how much weight Lassiter throws around here. I walked right in with Hopkins and Delaney yelling that I wasn't allowed here. But here I am."

"Craig, I want you to leave."

"I'm here for one reason. I'm taking you to town. We're getting married. *Today*."

She shook her head so violently that some of the

dark red hair she had done up began to tumble. "I will not marry you!"

"You'll change your mind in a damn big hurry!"

He grabbed her by the wrist with such force that it caused her to scream. The kitchen door swung open and grim-faced Senna came a few steps into the parlor, with a sawed-off shotgun in her hands.

"This belonged to my man, bless his soul," she said in a husky voice. "An' it'll shoot just as straight as when he was alive. Now you do what Mrs. Borling said. You git!" She gestured toward the door with the twin barrels of the Greener.

Moran stiffened and gave her a long look, saying, "I'll remember this, Senna." He flung Delira a cold glance. "Also, I won't forget this day with you!"

He went slamming out of the house. Three men on horses were at the foot of the veranda steps. Ignoring them, he swung into the saddle and spurred away. The men followed to make sure he crossed the Muleshoe line.

He rode in a fury to where he had left Joplin and the others. His face was livid.

"Joplin, do you think you can find the place where you left the kid?"

"Sure. But he'll be gone from there."

"We can track him. Let's go."

That was hours ago. Shortly after Moran left, Senna went to town for the mail. She returned with a bulky letter from Jim Sloan, the sheriff, written from the territorial capital.

To occupy her seething mind, Delira read the letter

156

again, sensing the sheriff's sincerity even though she scoffed at his flowery language. As if that would impress her.

Well, he wasn't so bad-looking, she realized, conjuring up his image. He was older than she'd like for a mate but tough enough and reliable. People seemed to like him. But even as the possibility of Sloan as a husband crossed her mind, she hurled the letter at a window. Three pages of flowery script fluttered to the floor like shot birds.

She had sought to lure Lassiter to her side, believing that only a minimum of her charm would be needed. But all he seemed to be interested in was the boy—not her, but Rance Borling. Damn Lassiter!

After her outburst, she began to calm down and wonder about the boy. Had Moran killed him? He was quite capable of such an act, she was sure. For the first time she felt a shred of pity for the boy. He had always been in the way, and Timmie had devoted what she thought was far too much attention to his son. Plain jealously on her part, she supposed. The thought put a tight smile on her lips.

Crossing the room, she picked up Jim Sloan's letter, folded it and put the three sheets in a pocket of her dress. She didn't want Senna to get her hands on it. To pass the time, she began thinking again about Sloan as a husband. She sensed that he was probably a man easy to fool at those times when her hot blood stirred her into seeking adventures. Yes, she could do worse than marry Jim Sloan.

With her limited knowledge of finances, Sloan

would be a great help. He must have kept the records of his sheriff's office straight, so he should be capable of handling Muleshoe. Since Timmie had been in prison, Moran had drained the bank account in Hopeville. All the money she had left was in the safe, and there was precious little of that.

Moran and his men were just riding out of a deep gorge. Straight ahead was a natural stone bridge, a great sweep of rock from one canyon rim to another. As they topped a rise, black-bearded Sam Dirk suddenly reined in. He pointed down into a valley thick with aspen. Just crossing a clearing were several riders.

"Looky," Dirk said with a fierce grin. "It's Lassiter, sure as hell!"

Moran looked and recognized the jaunty figure in the saddle. Obviously, they hadn't found the boy and from their slow pace he judged they were tracking him.

"Where'd you leave the kid from here?" Moran demanded of Joplin.

"North," Joplin answered, pointing in that direction.

And Lassiter was traveling westward, which meant the lost kid was traveling farther and farther away.

Joplin drew his rifle. "I can make a try at bringin' Lassiter down."

"Too far," Moran said through his teeth. "Besides, I want that bastard alive, if possible." He touched his spurs to his horse. "We'll get in behind 'em and watch our chance."

But it didn't quite work out the way Moran had planned. Lassiter made a break from his men and eventually located the boy.

# Chapter Sixteen

Instead of taking Rance to Muleshoe, Lassiter, keeping his eyes open for Moran and his men, went on to Hopeville. Down a side street under an arch of trees he finally came to a pair of adjoining buildings. A sign in front: JOSHUA STEENBOLT, M.D.

All the many miles Rance had suffered greatly because of the jolting ride that pounded his broken leg. He had passed out again. Lamplighted windows assured him the doctor was home.

Lassiter carefully got him down from the horse, carried him to a porch and kicked at a front door with his boot.

Steenbolt, a tall, Lincolnesque man, opened the door, looking annoyed that someone had kicked it. The sight of Lassiter caused the annoyance to deepen and his bony shoulders stiffened.

"What do you want?" he said before he saw the boy in Lassiter's arms. He stood aside. "Bring him in."

"It's the Borling boy."

"What happened to him?"

"It's a long story. He was in the mountains . . . by himself. He fell. And this is the result."

Steenbolt led the way down a narrow hall to his office and small hospital that had been added to the house. He took a ring of keys from his pocket, selected one and unlocked the door. There was a stong smell of carbolic acid in the air.

He lit a lamp, took the boy from Lassiter and placed him on a bed. Deftly, the doctor undressed Rance.

"Thank God he's unconscious," Lassiter said fervently.

"He may not be for long. Hold him down, if you please."

Sweat popped out on the boy's forehead and he began to make whimpering sounds as the doctor set the broken leg and splinted it.

When he was finished and Rance tucked into bed, the doctor fingered his chin whiskers and regarded Lassiter coldly. "What, may I ask, was the boy doing in the mountains alone?"

Lassiter hesitated, wondering if the doctor would believe the truth. Steenbolt had been foreman of the jury that had found Timmie Borling and himself guilty of murder. And it had been admitted by their lawyer that Steenbolt had likely influenced his fellow jurors in reaching a guilty verdict. For some reason, Steenbolt had taken a violent dislike to him. And now there was no telling how he might twist the truth.

So Lassiter said, "The boy ran away."

"It doesn't appear that he had much supervision. I understand Mrs. Borling removed him from the Adderly house."

"She did. They . . ."

"My main concern now is for the young gentleman. Not in what the Adderlys did or did not do. Pass the word to Mrs. Borling that it might be wise for her to visit the boy. At her convenience, of course." The last was said thinly. The doctor's eyes glittered in the lamplight.

"I'll get word to her."

"I was sure you would."

It had been a long, hard day—hours in the saddle, being jumped by Moran and his men, the loss of Blanchard. And on top of that, finally finding the boy with a broken leg. Had he not been found, Rance wouldn't have lasted another day. The thought of it put a cold chill down Lassiter's spine. He faced the doctor.

"Look, I know you don't like me. But that's not important now. The main thing is to do all you can for the boy."

"I intend to," Steenbolt said stiffly. "And as for not liking you, I'm sorry you ever came to Hopeville in the first place. I'm certainly sorry you came back here after being condemned by your peers for murder."

"Later we were found to be innocent. For Borling, it was a little late, it seems."

"Since your return I've seen your handiwork. I treated a gunshot wound suffered by Petey Sagar. Inflicted by you. I also had Meager Joplin as a patient after the beating you gave him."

It took sheer willpower for Lassiter to hold himself in. "Just take care of the boy. Nothing else is important."

"My dear sister married such a man as you. A drifter. A gunman. A killer."

"Now wait a minute . . ."

"In fact, he even looked a little like you. He abandoned her and her baby. They did not survive. When you first arrived in Hopeville and I learned of your reputation, I hoped to find some way to get rid of you. Unfortunately, Timmie Borling took a liking to you."

"We were old friends."

Rance opened his eyes, smiled at Lassiter and extended a small hand from the covers. Lassiter walked over and took it in his own. The hand was hot.

"Thanks for . . . for finding me, Lassiter," Rance said in a voice barely above a whisper.

"You get to feeling better, Rance. It's all I ask."

Lassiter stepped out to the porch. The doctor followed him, closing the door.

"Now that you've thrown Craig Moran off Muleshoe, so I hear, I suppose you'll have your way again with Mrs. Borling."

"What the hell do you mean *again?*" Lassiter whispered, his anger spilling over at last.

"I saw the way you looked at her when you first came to work at Muleshoe. Everyone did."

"Timmie Borling was my friend. And the last thing I'd have done was go behind his back."

"I don't believe you."

Lassiter went to the Trail's End, so stirred up he hoped to run into Moran and settle the dirty business between them, once and for all. But the place was nearly empty. He had a drink, thinking of his confrontation with Steenbolt, whom few people called doc; he preferred "doctor." And no one, at least a second time, ever shortened Joshua to Josh. He was a stiff-necked fool and if there had been another doctor within a day's ride of Hopeville . . . he didn't finish the thought. The whiskey relaxed him, but he knew he shouldn't have another. What he wanted was sleep. He thought longingly of a room at the hotel, but knew he had to make the long ride out to Muleshoe to let Delira know that the boy was safe. There was always the possibility that beneath a brassy exterior there might be concern for Rance, however slight.

There was another reason why he felt obliged to return to Muleshoe. The threat of Moran and his men.

After passing through two of the guards he had set out, Lassiter, an hour later, was sprawled on the sofa in the Muleshoe parlor. He was sipping a glass of good whiskey. Delira was pacing up and down. She wore a blue wrapper and her hair bounced off her shoulders as she paced.

"I confess I never liked the boy," she said after he had related the day's happenings, "but I'm glad you found him and that he's safe."

"I wish there was another doctor, but Steenbolt's all we have."

"I sense he disapproves of me," Delira said with a toss of her head. Then she halted in front of Lassiter, her hands on her hips. Bending over, she studied him in the lamplight, her voice suddenly softer as she said, "You look all done in."

"It's been a helluva day." He thought he might as well give her the rest of it. "We lost Blanchard."

"I'm sorry about that." He was surprised to see her chin tremble. As he watched her, he wondered if she was putting on, the way her eyes were squeezed shut, or was she genuinely touched by the passing of one of her men?

She asked for details about the killing and as he talked, she came to sit beside him on the sofa. He felt her warm thigh against him. Somehow the belt of the wrapper had come loose, which produced gaps in the garment.

The next thing he knew the tip of her warm tongue was exploring his ear. Then her lips were against his neck, her teeth nibbling him. Suddenly, she swung herself around so that she lay back across his lap, her fingers laced behind his strong neck. There was a mistiness in her eyes and her breathing quickened.

"Lassiter," she whispered huskily. And before he could respond, she fastened her mouth to his. Her lively tongue, which had seduced his right ear, now probed deeply into his mouth. He felt himself stir, despite his weariness, and the thought raced through his head, why not? Timmie was dead and there was no chance to make him a cuckold now.

Sweeping her into his arms, he carried her upstairs and dropped her onto the bed in her room. As she bounced, she squirmed out of the wrapper to reveal a nightgown of pure silk embroidered with small rose petals.

She reached out for him, her back arched as she whispered, "Oh . . . how wonderful. You are everything I imagined."

He was pulling off his shirt when he said, "What if Senna comes prowling?"

"She wouldn't *dare!*" Delira's eyes were shining.

"I've always sensed there was something savage about you, Lassiter," she whispered against his face. "Tonight be one."

And he was, all his frustrations, worry over the boy, the rest of it pouring out of him.

Finally, she lay back, a sheen of sweat upon her forehead. She was breathing hard as if from running a great distance.

"We'll have more nights like this, Lassiter, many more."

In the morning he overslept. He left Delira still asleep and crept downstairs. Senna was up, dusting in the parlor.

"Breakfast?" she asked, with no expression on her plump face.

"Find a small mule to cook. I'm that hungry." But she failed to smile at his attempted humor.

Ellick and Billings and Delaney had brought in Blanchard's body. That morning there was a funeral of sorts. Delira, looking lovely in green, read a passage from *Psalms* and Blanchard was laid to rest in the Muleshoe graveyard.

"With you at my side, Lassiter," Delira said, "I feel that nothing can touch me."

She spoke as they were walking back to the house. There he told her of his plans for roundup.

"There's no telling what Moran might try next," Lassiter said grimly. "So I think it'd be a good idea if you and Senna stayed in the Muleshoe suite at the hotel till roundup's over."

"If you think it's best," she responded with a warm smile. The ease with which she agreed surprised him.

"And look in on the boy every day while I'm gone," he suggested.

"I would have done that even without your telling me." She touched his hand and said, "We're going to be good partners."

When he made no reply he saw her frown. But he couldn't help it; he wasn't ready to commit himself.

That day the crew spent in getting the chuckwagon ready, and extra horses for the remuda brought in from pasture. Some of them had to have the hell worked out before they were fit once again for saddle work.

Late in the day, Delira asked Lassiter to come up to the house. Senna had brought the buggy around in front and sat waiting. She was to take Delira to the hotel in town as Lassiter had suggested.

Delira met him at the door with a lingering kiss. "So you won't forget me," she said, her eyes bright with promise.

"I'll never forget you." And he meant it. She was a tornado. In contrast, Ellen Stencoe was a placid summer breeze. But more reliable by far; he would bet on that.

As he rode out with his men, the chuckwagon creaking along, his thoughts were on Ellen. These past few days he should have stopped in at the hotel to see her. But one thing and another had intervened.

But the minute roundup was finished, he would see her, he vowed.

It was decided to work the north range first—start a

gather of saleable beef and push it gradually toward the home place. A sale of beef was imperative in order to keep the ranch in operation because, according to the books, their cash was dangerously low. Fortunately, he had heard of a ready market for cattle at Fort Smiley, only a little over a hundred miles to the east. Not much of a cattle drive these days. He could make it easily in a little over a week.

Lassiter was heartened when after the first day, a rough tally showed nearly five hundred head in the gather. It had been a year since the last Muleshoe roundup and in the meantime cows had drifted and gotten smarter. Some were hard to chase from their sanctuaries of brush or towering rocks or deep canyons. The only terrain really rough to work were the mountainous stretches of the Muleshoe range. He was shorthanded, but he decided to make do with what he had. They were all hard workers, top men with a catch rope or branding iron.

One day he ran into a gaunt man, Adams, just returning from a visit to Hopeville. He ranched some sections north of Muleshoe.

"How're things in town?" Lassiter wanted to know, intending to swing the conversation around to Craig Moran.

Si Adams tipped back his hat from a gray thatch and shook his head. "Seems like every man and many a boy are packin' guns these days."

"For what reason?"

"Folks are tight-lipped and wary. Like they was in the middle of a giant powder keg an' some fool was about to start tossin' matches about." Adams squinted at Lassiter. "Mostly folks worry about you an' Craig Moran bein' the ones to toss the matches."

"Did you see Moran while you were in town?"

"Nope."

Adams lifted his hand and rode on, soon to vanish in a sea of brush. The next time Lassiter looked, after chasing an ornery cow from a clump of pines, Adams was a mere speck against the horizon where the sky was already shot with the red flags of coming sunset.

At the end of the first week, one of the branders broke a leg when his horse stumbled and fell on him. Time was lost while one of the men rode him to town.

Lassiter questioned the man he had sent to accompany the injured party to the doctor's. Barney Delaney was round-faced with protruding eyes.

"How's Rance coming along?"

"Fine, so the doc says."

"What else did he say?"

"That he's puttin' on weight, for one thing." Delaney rubbed his square jaw and said, "Heard stories about Moran hirin' on some men."

"We'll keep our eyes open," Lassiter promised grimly.

The monotony of the roundup continued—throwing the Muleshoe brand on any unbranded cattle, wrestling calves away from their mothers. Smoke of branding fires stained the clear sky. Men sweated and swore and grumbled but at night they relaxed after eating the meals cooked up by Billings.

Around a campfire one night, Lassiter remarked that working roundup on Muleshoe wasn't as rough as doing likewise in the Texas brush country where he had spent one spring. Ellick, resting against a chuck-wagon wheel, his long legs outstretched on the ground, laughingly agreed. As a kid he had worked for his old man south of San Antone. He still had traces of what he called his "How y'all" accent.

Night guards were always out to watch the herd, relieved every four hours. So far, all had gone well. Almost too well, was the way Lassiter figured it. That Moran hadn't made a move bothered him. It wasn't like the man to give up so easily.

Usually after supper a harmonica would come out of Delaney's pocket. He would sit by the dying fire, his face ruddy in the flames, and blow sweet music. Sometimes the men would sing along with him and other times they'd just settle back and listen, each with his own private thoughts.

Each night before rolling up in his blanket—unless he had first watch—Lassiter would ride around the camp, his rifle loose in the scabbard, his eyes piercing the shadows for signs of suspicious movement. It worried him that he saw nothing.

# Chapter Seventeen

When Ellen Stencoe tried to be friendly with Delira Borling, she was rebuffed. Senna caught a dejected Ellen on the hotel veranda and patted her on the arm.

"Don't you pay no mind to Mrs. Borling," she advised. "She's got a lot to think about. Mainly that fella Lassiter." Senna tittered, then glanced over her plump shoulder to be sure no one else was around. Turning back to Ellen, she said, "Mrs. Borling, she's sweet on Lassiter, if you ask me. More than she's been with any of the others."

If Senna noticed the sudden change her words had brought to Ellen's face, she made no comment, but wheeled about and lumbered into the hotel.

Ellen stood for a long time, clinging to the veranda railing until her fingers ached, staring off at cliffs that rose into the sky north of town, but in reality seeing nothing. What the woman had said was very upsetting. Would Lassiter be able to stay out of the grip of such a determined female as Delira Borling? she wondered.

She had another shock that day when she joined

many of the locals, with nothing better to do, and watched the arrival of the twice-weekly northbound stagecoach. It helped take her mind off herself and Lassiter by watching for the first sign of dust in the distance and hearing the first shout, "Here she comes!"

She watched the banner of dust come closer, generated by whirring wheels and hooves of the six-horse team. Minutes later it came roaring and swaying into town to pull up in front of the hotel, causing a great cloud of dust that lifted high, then began to settle. The first passenger to alight was a thin woman with two small children who were met by a bearded man. They went off, arm in arm, the children dancing happily around them.

The scene of family bliss brought a wistful smile to Ellen's lips. In her mind she pictured the scene in her own life; if all went well she would have two children, a boy and a girl, only it would be Lassiter who went away and who was met when the stage pulled in. He would have gone, say, to a cattleman's convention and she and the children would be on hand to greet him.

Her dream was abruptly shattered when the next passenger stepped down. He was tall and raw-boned and carried a saddle by the horn in one hand, a rifle in the other. A bedroll was draped over his shoulder. Her jaw fell.

"Ralph!" she exclaimed so loudly that his head snapped around and he stared at her up on the hotel veranda.

"Ellen!" He looked angry as he came thumping up the veranda steps two at a time. He dumped his saddle and bedroll on the porch at her feet and put down the rifle. She stood numbly, staring.

"Ralph," she finally managed to say as he glared, "what in the world are you doing here?"

"I got your letter."

"I see. . . ."

"I told Saunders I wanted a leave, but he wouldn't give it so I quit right then and there."

"You quit your job?" She was horrified. "But it was such a good job."

The face of Ralph Benson, who was tall and lean and well-muscled, was slowly reddening. "I had to see for myself." He glanced at those who had come to witness the arrival of the stage. "Where's this Lassiter hombre?" Benson demanded. "He around?"

"He . . . he's working roundup at Muleshoe . . . up in the mountains."

"You married to him yet?"

"Why . . . why no."

"Why not?"

Bewildered by the barrage of questions, she felt at a loss. But only for a few moments, then she stiffened her spine.

"Mainly because he hasn't asked me, if you must know."

"I thought so," he said in a hard voice.

"I'm very disappointed in you, Ralph, that you took it upon yourself to . . . to check up on me. And that's what it amounts to. Snooping." Her chin was jerking and tears beginning to sting her eyes. Several people had turned to look at them, nudging one another.

She tried to pull on his arm, to get him to move where they wouldn't be noticed, but he stood with feet spread, refusing to budge.

172

"I've known you most of my life, Ellen, an' the first time you go away, you let some hombre put a ring in your nose an' lead you around like a pet calf."

"That's not a very nice thing for you to say, Ralph." Angrily, she brushed at tears beginning to fall down her cheeks.

But Ralph Benson didn't wait for her to finish. He shouldered his bedroll, snatched up saddle and rifle and was stalking down the veranda steps. She saw him heading toward a sign: HOPEVILLE LIVERY STABLE.

As if frozen, she watched him stride into the building, wondering if she should go after him, to try to get him to see that she was truly in love. That her feelings for Lassiter were genuine, not just some passing fancy.

While she was trying to make up her mind, he came riding out on a chestnut, tall in the saddle, his jaw outthrust, the hat on the back of his head to reveal a thatch of wiry hair. He didn't ride past the hotel but instead went along an alley. She leaned far over the railing and called to him. But either he failed to hear her or chose to ignore the plea.

She watched him with a heavy heart until he was out of sight. Why did Ralph have to come here? she asked herself. She wiped her eyes. Flooding through her mind were memories of their times together, the soft pressure of his lips.

Why was her life so complicated all of a sudden?

As she stood there at one end of the hotel veranda, she was suddenly frozen with terror as she realized Ralph's probable destination. Until now her mind had been in such turmoil she hadn't been thinking straight.

He was going to confront Lassiter, of course. He

had rented a livery stable horse, would ride to Muleshoe and there learn the approximate location of the roundup camp.

"Oh, my God . . ."

Lifting her skirts, she fled down the veranda steps and along the alley Ralph had taken. A woman removing clothes from a line in a yard looked at her in amazement, a frantic girl, dark hair streaming out from the knot at the back of her head.

Finally, out of breath, a pain in her side, Ellen had to stop. Ralph was out of sight. She put her hand on a high board fence until she could get her breath back, then she turned back for the hotel.

Before Ralph's arrival in Hopeville she had been so certain. But suddenly she was torn with doubt. Even though faint, the doubt was there and could not be denied, like a dull pain.

But she had given herself to Lassiter and was committed now. There was to be no reopening of old gates. Having reached that determination, her chin came up. All she could pray for now was that the meeting between Lassiter and Ralph would be peaceful.

She washed her face at the hotel, and, as she had been doing each day, she walked to the Steenbolt residence. Rance, propped up in bed, greeted her enthusiastically as usual. Since his injury she had taken it upon herself to act as his tutor to make up for the lessons he was missing at school. That night at her brother's place, Lassiter had told her how fond he was of the boy.

Although not planned this way, the school teaching

days she thought had been left back in Tucson were with her again.

"How are you today, Rance?"

"Comin' along fine. I can walk a little. Want to see me?"

"You bet I do."

# Chapter Eighteen

It had been a rough day at roundup. A steer had gored Ellick's horse and he had been thrown hard. He had been shaken up, but was ready to go back to the saddle. Then an hour later Billings had been flattened by a raging cow when he tried to separate her from a calf. In the monotony of their job a man sometimes got careless. And that had happened to Billings. For just a second he forgot that a cow could be much more dangerous at times than a bull because it charged with eyes open while a bull closed his. Even though at the last minute he'd tried to sidestep, the cow struck him with her head. In trying to break his fall, Billings had sprained both wrists. They were swelling.

"Christ, what next?" an exasperated Lassiter exclaimed, as he stared at the branding fires, the restless cattle in the gather that had to be watched every minute. Another day here and they'd move camp. All the men were worn to the bone, Lassiter included. But he never let on.

It was midafternoon when a rider approached and asked Billings if Lassiter was around. Billings indicated Lassiter, who had just brought in a bunch of steers for the gather and had dismounted to take a pull at one of the big canteens kept by the chuckwagon.

He set down the canteen and curiously watched the stranger approach, a tall man probably in his midtwenties. Or maybe a little older. It was hard to tell. He had a face bronzed from the sun that made his blue eyes seem intense, and had lightened the hair seen below his hat brim. He looked the type to usually wear a warm smile but today his lips were tight. Lassiter sensed a seething anger the man was trying hard to suppress. But Lassiter knew it couldn't be directed against him for he had never seen the man before.

"Heard you might be hirin', Lassiter," the stranger said bluntly. "I can use a job."

"Can you cook?"

"Tolerably well," he responded with some surprise. "But I'm a better cowhand."

"My cook's got two bad wrists so he's out of it for now. What's your name?"

"Benson, Ralph Benson."

He stood with teeth clenched, hands balled into fists as if halfway expecting Lassiter to make something out of the name. Lassiter explained the terms of employment. Fifty and food for roundup. Then if he wanted to stay on steady it would drop to forty.

Some of the evident tension seemed to ease out of Benson. He said, "Suits me. What you want me to do?"

Lassiter set him to working cattle. Toward sundown,

177

Benson knocked off riding, built up the cook fires and prepared a meal. For supper that twilight they had fried steak, beans and tinned tomatoes.

"You'll do, Benson," Lassiter complimented him with a smile. But the man only shrugged and returned to his tin plate heaped with food.

After supper when the men lounged around smoking, Lassiter said quietly, "You act like a fella who's got plenty on his mind. You running from something?"

"Nope."

"How come you came up here?"

"Just got an itch to study the country an' . . . things." Benson's hard eyes settled momentarily on Lassiter's face. Then he looked away.

Each man was responsible for his own plate. Over the sounds of tin plates being sanded on the creek bank where they were camped, Lassiter said, "Best to get things off your mind, Benson. It turns a man sour to carry things too long in his craw."

Benson's reaction took Lassiter by surprise. The man leaped to his feet and stood over him in a menacing posture.

"All right," he snarled. "You kept on pushin' me so I'll tell you what's stuck in my craw so bad it's like a giant toothache."

Sensing trouble, Lassiter got slowly to his feet, dropped his cigarette and stepped on it. All the men were staring.

"All right, Benson, speak your piece."

"You figure to marry with Ellen Stencoe?"

The question took Lassiter by surprise. "I don't figure to marry anybody. And what business is it of yours?"

"I'll tell you what business it is of mine!" Benson was yelling, nearly out of control.

Billings, sitting with his two swollen wrists in his lap, looked worried. "Watch it, Lassiter."

And staring at the younger man, Lassiter suddenly got it. Ralph Benson. Hadn't Ellen mentioned her betrothed by that name?

"Hey, wait a minute, Benson!"

Lassiter saw the shift of Benson's shoulder and knew he was going to be hit. But he managed to pull aside just enough so that the fist only grazed a cheekbone instead of hitting him head-on.

Lassiter swung his fist and missed, because Benson was jumping around. Teeth bared, his blond hair loose about his head, Benson looked like an avenging Greek god. Those who were supposed to be guarding the herd rode close to watch the excitement.

Lassiter was sparring with Benson by then, slashing a right into the midsection that produced a great whoosh.

But Benson danced away, a grayness in his face now because he was hurting.

"Goddamn you, Lassiter, leadin' on a sweet girl like Ellen an' . . ."

In his rage he lunged. It was the wrong move because Lassiter was already swinging toward the jaw. Benson's momentum only intensified the force of the blow. He straightened up, his blue eyes suddenly crossed, and came down in a heap beside the cook fire. Lassiter

179

stooped and dragged him away from the flames.

"Crazy damn fool," he muttered, rubbing the knuckles of his right hand; one of them was split.

Kneeling, he splashed water from a canteen into Benson's face, then gave him a drink.

"I hope you got it out of your system," Lassiter remarked with a faint grin. But Benson just stared at him.

"I don't know where Ellen got the idea that we'd marry," Lassiter went on. But suddenly it came to him, guiltily. He did know. It was because of the night they had spent together out at her brother's place, the late Bert Stencoe who was said to have written out a confession then blown his head off with a shotgun. Lassiter swore at himself because of that night with Ellen. Why had he been so foolish? he asked himself and stared at Benson in the shadows. It was nearly dark.

"I'll be goin'," Benson said, starting to get up. But Lassiter pulled him back.

"Soon as roundup's over, let's you and me face Ellen together."

"Like I said, I'll be goin'. You won't want me around after me tryin' to brain you."

"You got money coming for a day's work."

"Hell with it."

"I'm asking you to stay on. I'm shorthanded."

While Benson seemed to be thinking it over, his brows knitted in a scowl, there came a sudden chorus of yells at the far edge of the herd. This was followed by a crackle of gunfire.

Lassiter grabbed his rifle and fired twice in the general direction of the shouting. He was rewarded by a man's yelp of pain.

Then the steers, poised one minute with heads up, as if listening to the commotion, suddenly broke into a mad run.

*"Stampede!"* Lassiter yelled and ran for his horse.

By the time Lassiter hit the saddle, the very ground was shaking as if from a cataclysm. Through the filmy darkness now filled with dust, he saw a lead steer lose its footing and somersault through the air, its legs jerking. Other steers hard on the heels of the unfortunate animal began to pile up, resulting in a growing mound of squalling, injured cattle. Another rifle shot splintered the side of the chuckwagon that Lassiter was passing.

At a hard run, he got off a one-handed shot with his Henry. And the rifleman, aiming directly at Lassiter, this time was knocked off the back of his plunging horse. He began to run frantically, waving his arms as if that would divert the flood of enraged animals so close on his heels. As Lassiter watched helplessly, the man went under, his screams briefly heard above the roar of hooves. Lassiter spurred hard to outrun the wave of bellowing animals.

"Turn 'em! Turn 'em!" Lassiter was shouting, now far enough ahead so that he could bring pressure to bear on the leaders. They dripped froth from their mouths, their eyes wild as they were gripped solidly by the insanity of stampede. But gradually he began to turn the leaders. A rider was pounding along at his side, his blond hair flying. It was Ralph Benson, whose hat hung down the back of his neck, secured by a chin strap.

"We're gettin' 'em!" he yelled over at Lassiter.

And Lassiter nodded in agreement. Gradually, they slowed the great mass of cows that were beginning to turn.

Billings, with his sprained wrists, was mainly guiding his sweated horse by pressure of the knees. Ellick was waving his rifle in the faces of the lead steers. It was a good five miles from the start of the ambush before they got the cattle milling and then halted completely.

Lassiter was breathing hard. His mouth was dry and his heart pounded.

"It was that son-of-a-bitch Moran who started it," Lassiter said angrily.

"Who's he?" Benson wanted to know. But Lassiter didn't feel like filling him in and left it up to Ellick.

With dust from the stampeding cattle no longer a hazard, the moonlight was strong enough so he could backtrack along a giant swath that had been cut through the purple sage by the panicked animals. A giant roadway smashed by flying hooves all the way from the ridges on down to the flats. Lassiter came upon the ruins of the chuckwagon that lay in many pieces as if smashed in a fit of anger by a giant's fist.

He found one of his men, Joe Crombie, his body ground to a pulp but the skull, with its reddish beard, miraculously spared.

They managed a few hours of sleep, finally, taking turns at guard duty. But the herd had run itself out and stood spraddle-legged, heads down. No more running for them this night. But there was always the possibility that Moran would strike again. However, he didn't.

When it came time for Lassiter to take a turn as

guard he found himself paired with Ralph Benson. The side of Lassiter's face still ached where Benson's knuckles had grazed him. After several circlings of the herd, Benson rolled a cigarette as he talked.

"I'll be headin' back home on the next southbound," he announced, avoiding Lassiter's eyes. Moonlight spilled a yellow cast over the exhausted cattle. A swift tally had showed the loss to be around two dozen head. There had been Joe Crombie as a Muleshoe casualty. And one of Moran's men had gone down under the flailing hooves. But Lassiter couldn't tell who it was because the features were unrecognizable.

"Have a talk with Ellen," Lassiter said. "Pick up where you left off."

"Not that easy. She's different. Changed ever since she got a letter from the sheriff sayin' her brother confessed to murder then shot himself."

"Ellen came up here to find out about her brother," Lassiter reminded. "Craig Moran tried to blame her brother's death on me, but I set her straight on that."

"Yeah, she told me." There was a faint edge to Benson's voice as his eyes lanced through the moonlight to fasten on Lassiter's face.

"Well, she knows the story now so take her home."

"Well, I'll be goddamned," Benson said softly. "A girl gives you her heart an' you step on it."

Lassiter found Benson's penetrating blue eyes were making him uncomfortable, compounding his feeling of guilt because of his night with Ellen Stencoe.

"I'm telling you again," Lassiter said in a hard voice to mask his feelings. "Take her back to Tucson with you."

"What if she won't go?"

"It's up to you to talk her into it."

"I see you don't know Ellen very well. Nobody puts her in harness."

"You can sway her . . . if you halfway try." Lassiter's temper was beginning to slip. It had been a long and dangerous night and he was out of sorts at the loss of a man, the lesser loss of cattle.

"I had almost started to admire you, Lassiter. The way you handled the stampede an' all." Benson was hunched in the saddle, regarding Lassiter in a flood of moonlight, the unlit cigarette dangling from a corner of his mouth.

Lassiter thumbed a match, leaned in the saddle with the flame toward Benson. But the younger man drew back and lit his own. Lassiter applied the flaming match to his cigarette, whipped out the flame and dropped it on the ground. Tobacco smoke burned his lungs and it came to him that a man was a fool to poison his body with raw smoke. But he knew he'd continue doing so till the day they put him under the ground.

"Yeah, if you'd said, 'I love her an' want to marry her.' Sure, I'd have been hurt, but I'd say to myself if that's what she really wants, then that's that. But you don't do that. All you say is, 'Take her back to Tucson.' In other words, get rid of her. She's a bother."

"Goddamn it, Benson! It isn't that way at all!"

At that moment Billings, with his sprained wrists swathed in bandages, came riding up with Ellick to relieve them.

By the time Lassiter awakened in the morning, Benson was gone. Good riddance, Lassiter thought. Then in the next breath he felt sorry for the man.

Because all their supplies had been ground into the earth by pounding hooves, a buck deer was shot. They feasted on venison for breakfast.

After eating, they buried Crombie. Then, short-handed, they started the remainder of the herd on the long drive to the fort where the Army would take over.

It took them all of a week to make the drive. Then, with a bank draft buttoned in his shirt pocket, Lassiter and his men started back over the mountains to Hopeville.

# Chapter Nineteen

Ralph Benson took to brooding, drinking too much at the Trail's End. From things Benson had been saying, Moran surmised the reason for the demon on his back.

During Lassiter's absence, several plans had passed through Craig Moran's mind. He could burn down the buildings at Muleshoe, for one thing, which would teach Delira a lesson. But easy as that seemed at the moment, there were several things against such an act. In the first place, there was public opinion. Hopeville was about evenly divided concerning Lassiter, he had learned. Those against him for the most part were silent, but those who favored him were vocal in their support.

In addition to getting probably half the valley against him, Moran knew burning out Muleshoe would be a foolish move. It would take months to replace the buildings. And he needed a bunkhouse for the full crew he expected to hire. It was all a matter of backing Delira into a corner and forcing a ring on her finger.

However, there was always the matter of Lassiter,

who loomed like a giant shadow over his plans. But he was through playing games with Lassiter, such as having his men pinned down in the mountains, interrupting their hunt for the boy. And later, setting off the stampede, which had cost him two men. One of them was fairly easy to identify, but the other ground forever into the soft ground by hooves of the frenzied steers.

His best bet, he decided after thinking it over, was to call Lassiter in front of witnesses. Let him go for his gun and beat him. He was confident he could do it. But to give himself a winning edge, he would let Joplin and Petey Sagar get into it. He would say later to the witnesses that the pair had such a hatred for Lassiter that it was impossible for them to hold themselves back, which was all too true so far as the hatred went.

When Lassiter was halfway home from the cattle drive, Sheriff Jim Sloan returned suddenly from his business trip to the territorial capital. He alighted from the southbound in midafternoon, wearing a new gray suit and smoking a cheroot, the smoke curling from under the brim of his new hat.

He looked slim and fit. The first thing he learned upon his return was that Delira Borling was living at the hotel in the company of her cook and maid, Senna.

Sloan knocked discreetly on the door of her suite, told her who it was and saw the door swing open. He didn't know quite what to expect after his long romantic letter to her, but he wasn't prepared for anger.

"Hello," she said. "Have you seen or heard from Lassiter?" she demanded bluntly and stepped aside to let him enter. Senna bulked in the doorway of the second room of the suite for a moment, then stepped back and closed the door.

"You mean Lassiter is still in these parts?" Sloan asked with a frown.

"Don't look so surprised. I miss him something terrible." She hugged herself and waltzed around the room while Sloan sat stiffly at the edge of the sofa watching her.

"Yeah, I guess I'm a little surprised." Sloan eased the bind of his new trousers at the knee. "I figured he'd be gone by the time I got back."

"No such thing. He's staying on at Muleshoe, working for me." Her eyes danced. She waltzed to a front window that overlooked Center Street and peered down at the street below.

His mouth gradually hardened as he thought of Lassiter in connection with the luscious female who stood with her back turned so he could see the width of gentle shoulders outlined in some kind of gauzy material of her dress, the way it dipped at her waist and tightened over shapely hips. He felt his heart begin to pound and his mouth was suddenly dry. When he thought of Lassiter touching her, he turned cold.

Oh, he had guessed, along with everyone else, about her involvement with Craig Moran in the past. But that was different somehow. Lassiter owed him, dammit. He could kick himself now for having felt sorry for Lassiter, believing him innocent of having a hand in the murder of Dave Ashburn. He—Jim Sloan—had made it possible for Lassiter to get out of Rimshaw Prison. But he had thought that Hopeville would be the last place Lassiter would want to visit after his release, in view of the humiliation he had suffered here. Being accused of murder, sentenced after a quick trial and carted off to prison where it was intended he would waste his young manhood and end up an ancient derelict in twenty-five years. Provided he was able to withstand the monotony and brutality of the prison.

"You got my letter?" he asked tentatively.

She turned and faced him, saying, "Oh, yes. But my mind these days is so filled with Lassiter I couldn't give it much thought."

Delira was pleased to note that her words twisted his lean face in agony. "I'm very much in love with Lassiter," she went on as if that would make everything all right. "Oh, but I have some competition. Foolish Ellen Stencoe thinks she has him. But she hasn't." Delira's chin came up. "Naturally, if you compare the two of us you can see why."

"I . . . I had hoped you'd give my letter some consideration," he said gravely, trying to keep the hurt from his voice. He stared at a bar of sunlight across an Indian rug at his feet.

"It was a beautiful letter and I was touched. I really was. But under the circumstances, there is no chance for you."

"Because of Lassiter."

"Precisely."

Slowly he got to his feet, holding his hat. "Maybe you'd better not count too much on Lassiter."

Her eyes snapped at him. "What do you mean by that?"

"He's got a rep as a drifter."

"Well, he won't drift from me, you can be sure of

that." She walked with him to the door. "I'm glad you're home, Jim."

"You are?" he asked with some surprise.

"I'm sure that when Lassiter gets back he'll want to talk to you about Craig Moran. He's done some devilish things since you've been away."

It was two days later that Sloan witnessed Lassiter's return to Hopeville with his men. A weary-looking, dusty lot. They slid from their tired horses and entered the Trail's End. Sloan soon elbowed up to the bar beside Lassiter, who shoved a bottle to the sheriff and called for a glass.

"Welcome home . . . to both of us," Lassiter said with a faint grin.

Sloan poured for himself, lifted his glass, his eyes locked with Lassiter's. "I hear you've become quite a ladies' man."

Lassiter's face darkened, his good humor vanished. "What's in your craw, Jim?" he asked in a low voice.

"You've got that Stencoe girl doing cartwheels. And Mrs. Borling is . . . is waiting to welcome you home."

Lassiter didn't miss the steel in the sheriff's voice. "I'll be pushing on soon as I get things straightened out for Borling's son at Muleshoe," Lassiter said.

"You mean that? About pushing on?"

"I do, Jim. I'd never have come back here in the first place if it hadn't been for the boy. Now that you're back, maybe we can have a talk about getting that lawyer, Curt Hanley, to make it all legal. I figure to be fair that half of Muleshoe should belong to Mrs. Borling and half to Rance."

The sheriff rubbed his jaw thoughtfully, then said,

"You could put in a clause to the effect that she forfeits it all if she ever remarries. That way Rance won't have a stepfather to browbeat him."

Lassiter studied the tight smile on the sheriff's lips, then said he'd think it over. But he thought the idea was cruel. To deprive Delira of the marriage bed would be the same as shooting full of holes the canteen of someone floundering through desert heat.

When Rance was first brought to the doctor's, for some days he couldn't get out of bed. Doctor Steenbolt had given him one of the small bedrooms reserved for recuperating patients. The boy grew restless and kept asking about Lassiter.

"If he keeps on going, it'll be good riddance," Steenbolt muttered, which caused Rance to cry out in protest.

After that, Doctor Steenbolt decided to keep his personal feelings to himself.

He was all smiles, however, when Mrs. Delira Borling came to see how the boy was getting along. He told her the truth, that the boy was progressing nicely but was restless.

"How long will he have to be here?" she asked crossly.

"That depends." He noticed that the handsome woman seemed very short-tempered these days.

As she was getting ready to leave, Ellen Stencoe knocked on the door. Delira's brows lifted as she saw the tall girl. Steenbolt hastily made introductions, which Delira imperiously waved aside.

"Miss Stencoe has been reading to the boy— tutoring him," Steenbolt explained.

Ellen flushed at the way Mrs. Borling was looking her over. "I am a schoolteacher. Or rather, I used to be. I hope you don't mind me tutoring Rance."

"Not at all. It's good for him. Good for me. Otherwise, I'd probably have to have him underfoot."

With that, she was gone, her hips swaying in a well-cut and expensive beige dress. Ellen had a feeling that Delira Borling cared nothing for Rance. She felt her heart go out to the boy.

As usual, the boy prefaced their meeting by wanting to know if she had heard from Lassiter. She shook her head. But she couldn't stem the rush of color to her face caused by the mere mention of his name. She knew he had much on his mind lately and when they did meet, usually accidentally, he seemed gruff. She had even begun to doubt that the night spent together had actually occurred.

Over the days a rapport developed between Ellen and Rance, with the boy's juvenile mind busy developing romantic dreams that included Ellen Stencoe and Lassiter. They would marry and he would go and live with them. The idea delighted him, but he kept it to himself.

Finally, he was able to hobble about on a crutch one of the hangers-on at the livery stable made for him. With the aid of the crutch he was soon able to hobble to the store where Ellen would buy him licorice, which he loved.

Twice Ellen saw Ralph Benson from a distance. Each time as she hurried forward to try in some way to heal the breach between them, he would see her, glare, and go quickly into the Trail's End. She was tempted to go in and confront him, but knew that would never do. As it was, she had become enough of a fallen woman because of Lassiter; to enter that type of establishment was unthinkable and would certainly destroy her reputation.

In some ways she almost wished she had never met Lassiter. Then she would be content with Ralph. But knowing Lassiter had been the highlight of her life; it was a memory she could never lose.

After his talk with the sheriff, Lassiter went to visit Rance at Doctor Steenbolt's. Rance was well and overjoyed to see him. He went on at great lengths how Ellen Stencoe was acting as his tutor. Lassiter said he was glad that Ellen was helping him pass the time.

As Lassiter was leaving, the doctor got him aside.

"You seem to genuinely care for the boy," Steenbolt said, fluffing out his whiskers.

Lassiter shrugged and put his hand on the doorknob.

"I guess that under the circumstances I've altered my opinion of you . . . to a point," the doctor went on.

Lassiter had to smile at the phrase "to a point." Steenbolt wouldn't let himself quite go all the way. "Take good care of the boy," Lassiter said in parting.

He had just stepped from the doctor's residence when he saw Senna plodding toward him, out of breath and perspiring.

"Mrs. Borling, she heard you was back an' she sent me to fetch you."

"I was on my way to the hotel, anyway," he told the woman who seemed unusually agitated.

"You best hurry 'cause she's all upset."

"I hear Ellen Stencoe is still in town."

"She is. Seen her this mornin'. . . ."

"I thought maybe she'd have gone back to Tucson."

"Now why'd she want to go an' do that?"

In the second-floor hallway of the hotel, Senna hurried ahead, flung open the door and fairly shouted, "I got him, Mrs. Borling, he's a-comin'."

"Senna, I want you to stay away for an hour, no make it two," came Delira's crisp voice from the room. "And when you do return, knock first. Knock real loud."

"Yes, ma'am."

Lassiter patted Senna on the shoulder as the woman stood aside so he could enter. Delira stood in the middle of the room, with a seductive smile on her lips.

"Shut the door, Lassiter," she said.

He took his time about closing it. Then, with his arms folded, he turned to face her. "You wanted to see me, I understand."

She gave a deep sigh. "Why didn't you come to me the moment you got back? I've been sitting here fretting . . ."

"I had things to do."

"You brought the money from the cattle sale?"

"The draft's been deposited in the bank. Did you think I'd steal it?"

"Oh, of course not." She stood with one hand on her hip, eyeing him. "Now that you're back, I'll return to Muleshoe. Rance is in good hands at the doctor's. Miss Stencoe is teaching him his numbers and his letters. By the way, she's quite attractive, don't you think?"

"Very," he answered with a sly smile.

"Oh, damn, why couldn't you have disagreed with

me?" Then, with her head back, she began to laugh but it died suddenly. She straightened up and said seriously, "I've been suffering since you've been away."

"I'm sorry to hear you've been ill," he said with a straight face.

"You know very well what I meant." She began to unbutton her dress at the side while breathing heavily, her eyes lancing his face. "Lock the door, if you will."

"Look, lady, when you climb down from that high saddle on that high horse, maybe I'll be willing to listen to you."

He went downstairs and knocked on Ellen Stencoe's door. Surprise and delight flooded her face when she saw him standing there, hat in hand. She asked him in but he shook his head.

"Haven't time. I just wanted you to know how much I appreciate what you've done for Rance. He likes you."

"And I like him. When will I see you, Lassiter?" He saw the small creases in the flesh between her fine eyes and winced. He looked both ways along the hallway, then lowered his voice. "Look, Ellen, that night never should've happened. Why don't you make it up with Ralph Benson?"

She slammed the door in his face. He stood for a minute, wondering what he should do, for he could hear her sobbing behind the door. But he decided to let her cry it out.

As he stepped from the hotel, a bank of clouds swirling in from the north swept in under the sun, dimming it. Because of the sudden shadow that fell over Hopeville and the rest of the range, he felt as if it might be a premonition of disaster. But he angrily thrust the idea aside, calling himself a fool to even think it.

Those men he had left behind at Muleshoe reported no trouble. Moran had not made a move, which was odd, Lassiter thought.

It was late afternoon when he was trying to make sense out of the Muleshoe books. There was a light tapping on the door. He was in the ranch office at the desk, ledgers stacked on shelves. There were two chairs and a sofa with a long rip where horse-tail stuffing was seeping out.

When he flung open the door he found Delira standing there, demure and chastened. "I'm sorry, Lassiter, for being such a bitch. But I worried so about you while you were gone . . . and I needed you so . . ."

She lightly kicked the door shut behind her and reached back to give the key in the lock a turn. At the moment she looked like a petulant schoolgirl.

"I'm trying to make things easier for you and the boy," he started to say.

"Especially for the boy?" She tilted her head, a small smile on her lips.

When he made no reply, her feet came sliding across the worn floor to finally reach the Indian rug where he was now standing. Gripping him by the arms, she looked up into his face.

"Make me a happy woman, Lassiter," she said seductively.

"I oughta turn you over my knee for the way you acted in town."

"Do that, too, if it'll make you happy."

"I'm not the kind who beats women to get pleasure."

"Even lightly?" She was teasing him now, running her hands in widening circles across his chest.

Then he took her in his arms, pressed his mouth down on hers. When she pulled away, her eyes were shining. Her plain white dress became a puddle of cotton fabric in the center of the room. Then she was undoing the lacings of her camisole.

In some ways it was better than their first encounter, more explosive. A cautioning voice far back in his mind warned him that Delira could become a dangerous habit that would be hard to break.

# Chapter Twenty

For a week, Lassiter and some of the crew moved cattle to better grass. He was working alone on the final day; the other men had returned to ranch headquarters. Hardly an hour passed since he had come back that Lassiter didn't wonder about Craig Moran. It bothered him that the man had not tried to make trouble. His last treachery had been to cause the stampede and that was nearly a month ago. Ellick said he had heard in town, via livery stable gossip, that Moran had gone south with his followers. But Lassiter wasn't convinced.

On this day, for one of the few times in his life, Lassiter grew careless. He had just pushed some dozen head of beef onto a grassy plot deep in a canyon. Taking a shortcut back to Muleshoe, he climbed a steep, shale-strewn trail to the rim of a canyon. This was a ridge topped by immense rocks of many twisted shapes that could in the creeping shadows be imagined as giant animals of a vanished age.

He was thinking about this while starting down the other side, a very steep trail in a defile, with numerous switchbacks below. In the growing twilight something made him look to his left. And in a flash he saw Petey Sagar in the saddle of a gray horse, his rifle stock tucked against his chin, grinning as he fired. That split second had given Lassiter time to ram in the spurs. But instead of bounding down the steep trail, his mount reared on its hind legs.

Above the crack of the rifle came the animal's shrill cry of pain. Lassiter felt a tremor run the length of the body. Already he was kicking free of the stirrups and drawing his rifle. But the horse, shot through the neck, dived off the trail and straight down, bumping the face of a cliff on the way.

Wind rushed past his face as he fell and it seemed as if his stomach were in a vacuum. Dropping the rifle, he blindly reached for a nub of brush that had taken root in a niche on the sheer rock wall. As his fingers snagged the tenuous margin of safety, his fall was checked. A sudden loss of momentum slammed him against the granite wall, almost dislodging his hold. Hanging by one hand, his fingers began to slip. Desperately, he maneuvered for a better hold. But his weight was too much. The whole gout of brush was torn loose. Dirt and pebbles rained down on him as he began to fall again. Directly below he spotted a narrow shelf and this time twisted his body in midair so as to make a precarious landing. Even then he barely kept his feet. But by sheer force of will, he was able to flatten himself against the canyon wall, no longer off balance. It also eased the strain on his teetering feet.

As he hugged the wall, he heard dim voices far above. At first, he couldn't make out what was being said, but gradually he picked up a word here and there and at last complete sentences.

". . . seen him go over the edge."

". . . light's bad down there, I can't see a thing."

"Hell, I nailed him dead center. Him an' his horse are a thousand feet down at the bottom of the canyon."

Lassiter recognized the voice of Petey Sagar. The other one might be Moran's but he couldn't be sure.

"Obviously, he's dead." It was definitely Moran. "That's all I give a good goddamn about. Good work, Petey."

"Time I finished off the bastard for him killin' my brother Rupe."

"Lassiter's dead!"

Delira, standing in the window of her bedroom, wearing the green wrapper, heard it from below. Leaning both hands on the windowsill, her heart beating coldly in her breast, she stared down. Some of her men were in a knot. She saw Petey Sagar and Joplin with them. And Moran, staring at her men as if daring them to do anything about his presence on Muleshoe.

"What did you say?" she called down to Ellick.

"Moran says Lassiter's dead, ma'am."

"Oh, he does, does he?"

She threw on a dress and was still buttoning it when she stormed down the stairs. Moran, his hat on the back of his head, looking devil-may-care with his broken nose and fierce grin, stood at the foot of the stairs. He had not even bothered to knock but had boldly entered the house.

"Who gave you permission to come in here?" she demanded, coming to a halt on the landing.

"You want to hear about Lassiter, don't you?"

"Whatever you're going to say, I won't believe."

This caused a stretching of lips so that his white teeth gleamed in the faint daylight in the entry hall where he stood. "Lassiter jumped us in the mountains and Sagar shot him. Lucky for us he did. Or Lassiter'd be the one standing here telling you *we* were the ones dead."

"Get out of here, Craig."

He started up the stairs.

*"Senna!"* she screamed.

That brought Senna bursting from the back part of the house, the sawed-off shotgun that had belonged to her late husband leveled at Moran.

He looked at the lumpy woman with contempt. "The next time you point that at me, it's going to be three feet down your throat." Then, lifting his head, he glared up at Delira frozen on the landing. "I'll be back," he threatened.

In a minute or so he and his men were riding past the windows. Ellick and her crew stood uncertainly in front of the house, watching them depart.

Delira ordered Senna to have the men hitch up the buggy, then she was to drive her to town.

It was past noon when they arrived in Hopeville with Senna driving directly to the sheriff's office. But Jim Sloan wasn't in. There was a sign in his office window stating that he would return around two o'clock.

Delira winced. Hammered by two blows already

today—learning of Lassiter's death and then on the heels of it, Moran's threat—she was not prepared for a third. She had expected Sloan to be available. In her suite at the hotel she penned a note, then when Senna came plodding in after having taken the buggy to the livery barn, ordered her to deliver it to the sheriff.

Buffeted by a mixture of fear and sorrow over Lassiter's passing, Delira walked with firm stride to the doctor's office. Ellen Stencoe, her hair pinned up, looking young and lovely, which only added to Delira's anger, was having Rance read to her from a primer. They were sitting on a bench beside the doctor's house in the warm sunlight.

Bluntly, Delira told Ellen about Lassiter, enjoyed seeing the swift drain of color from her young face.

"Oh, my God, are you sure?" Ellen finally managed.

Rance sat with mouth open, eyes filled with horror as he digested the tragic news. Tears began to trickle down his face, which he tried valiantly to wipe away so they wouldn't be noticed. Ellen leaned forward and held him. He sobbed against her breast.

"I'm the one who should weep," Delira said crossly when she noticed a shine of moisture at Ellen's eyes. "Lassiter and I were to have been married. My widowhood is at an end at last. But now . . ."

Ellen's head jerked around and she stared. "Married?" she gasped.

Delira gave her a cold smile. "If you'll leave us, Miss Stencoe, I have things to say to Rance. And, by the way, I think this ends your tutoring."

Ellen, trembling, dried her eyes, picked up her

pocketbook, gave Rance a pat on the shoulder and walked off.

Delira sat down on the bench. "You're leaving on the next southbound," she announced. "I picked out a school for you some months ago and now you're going to attend it."

"But . . . but I want to stay at Muleshoe."

"You'll do as I say!"

"But Lassiter said. . . ."

"I don't give one good goddamn what Lassiter said. He's no longer here to promote your welfare."

"He says Muleshoe is half mine an' I've got a right . . ."

Delira's right hand flashed, the palm of her hand cracking against the boy's cheek. His head rocked. But instead of busting into more tears he only looked at her steadily. This infuriated her.

"You little wretch," she hissed, "you've been a thorn in my side ever since I married your father."

She entered the doctor's house and spoke to Steenbolt, not knowing whether he had witnessed the scene from a window or not. She decided to cover herself just in case.

She spoke of how the boy's sass upset her so. "I . . . I just lose patience with him. His father could handle him but he's too much for a woman."

"Miss Stencoe seems to be able to get along with him," Steenbolt said gravely, his bearded lips barely stirring.

"She's had more practice." Delira forced a smile. "After all, she's been a school marm."

\* \* \*

The next day when Jim Sloan returned to town after a long ride and unlocked his office he found Delira's note slipped under the door.

> *Jim dear,*
>
> *I need you desperately.*
> *I'm at the hotel.*
>
> > *Your Delira*

The sight of the delicate feminine handwriting, the faint scent of her perfume on the paper, fired his blood. It came as no surprise that she needed him now that Lassiter was gone. And he knew she would use him if she could. But he was so madly infatuated with her that it didn't matter.

Folding the note carefully, he placed it in his pocket, gave it a pat, then made his way to the hotel.

She met him at the door and took his hands. They sat together on the small sofa. "It's so nice of you to come, Jim. You've heard about Lassiter?"

"I've been out since yesterday trying to find his body."

Her eyes flew wide. "You haven't found him?"

"Don't get your hopes up, Delira. He's very dead. We found his horse. But where he fell is a very deep canyon with many giant rocks. He could be on top of any number of them or in a crevice."

He went on to say that Moran had alerted him about Lassiter. It had been a shootout between Lassiter and Sagar.

"Then if you're friendly with Moran, I don't suppose you want to help me," she said tentatively.

Sloan was aware that her hand tightened on his. "I don't care much for Moran," he admitted. "But the man was straightforward enough to tell me about Lassiter. I have to give him credit for that."

"Moran . . . he's threatened me, Jim. I don't know what to do, so I turned to you . . . my only friend."

She looked imploringly up into his face, her gray eyes beginning to blur with tears. It seemed perfectly natural for him to lean down and kiss her on the mouth. And this very action brought her arms around his neck, pulling him down all the harder. What happened next was sheer instinct. He found his hands inside the front of her dress with Delira beginning to writhe on the sofa. Finally, she pushed his hands away and adjusted her dress.

"Please, Jim," she panted. "I . . . I want everything to be right for us. Let's wait . . . until . . ." She didn't finish it, but her eyes promised a new and exciting life that would take him out of his bachelorhood.

He found his heart squeezed and his mouth dry. Finally, he stood and picked up his hat. "I'll have a talk with Moran," he said huskily, looking down at her, so fragile, face flushed, on the sofa.

"Would you do that, Jim? For me? Honestly, I'm afraid of him. After your talk, come back. I'll be here."

When he had gone, she leaned against the door, her legs trembling. She could have let him have his way, but to tantalize him was better, she had decided. To pass the time, she called for the chambermaid to bring her the tub and plenty of hot water.

# Chapter Twenty-one

Out in the mountains, Lassiter had clung to the narrow ledge where he had been fortunate to land. It had taken him a few minutes to regain his breath. In the deep pools of shadow he began to inch his way along the ledge, hands on either side of his face flat against the wall that was still warm from the afternoon sun. At one point there was a three-foot break in the ledge where over the years it had crumbled and fallen away. Taking a deep breath, he gauged the distance and leaped. He came down lightly in perfect balance, clung a moment to the wall, then again began his descent.

It took him hours to reach the canyon floor. At one point he had had to swing from the trunk of a dwarf cedar growing from the cliff wall so he could land on a small promontory some fifteen feet below and to his left. It was a hard drop and he came crashing down, his feet stinging from the impact. He was thrown forward and skinned his knee.

But the pain was nothing. He was alive and that's all

that counted. Alive to hunt down the men who had tried to kill him.

He still had his .44, which, miraculously had remained in the holster, but his rifle was gone. Where in the maze of rocks had it landed? Even if could find it, which was unlikely even if he waited for daylight, after that hard fall it wouldn't be of much use anyway.

All the way down, there had been the ever-present danger of slipping and plunging to his death as had happened to his horse.

In the forest of giant boulders he started moving toward the east and south. By now, stars had taken form with the night and were blazing across the sky. Somewhere nearby an owl hooted and he heard the faint, distant roar of a mountain lion: There was only a hint of moon to the east to yellow the sky. He turned and looked back. High above loomed the shadowed rim of the canyon; he marveled at the distance of his precarious descent.

Finally, huddled against a tree, gun in his lap, he snatched a few hours of sleep. At daybreak he washed his face in a creek, then went searching for food. He found a big jackrabbit that spotted him too late. On the second bounding leap, a bullet from his .44 brought it down. Lassiter found moss and leaves and started a small smokeless fire. He broiled the meat, ate his fill, then started out again.

At last he came to the place where the Muleshoe gather had been stampeded. Here were the ruins of the chuckwagon and the great swath made in the acres of purple sage by the frenzied cattle. He passed the crude grave of the man lost and thought that it could be himself now lying in a slit in the ground instead of another man. Only dexterity, presence of mind and sheer luck had enabled him to escape the boiling mass of racing cattle. Mostly luck, he had to admit.

Much later he saw horsemen in the distance. He recognized Jim Sloan and Moran and Sagar and Joplin. Two other men he didn't know. It was tempting to call out and trust the sheriff to side with him. But could he be sure of Sloan? At the moment they were halted, letting their horses drink at a creek and Sloan was laughing at something Moran had said. Maybe not laughing too heartily, but laughing nevertheless.

He was close enough to hear his name mentioned, floating on the cool breeze to where he was supine in the brush, only his head lifted. He realized then that they were hunting for him, for his smashed body, no doubt.

They rode on.

It was the following day that Lassiter came in sight of Muleshoe headquarters, the big house he could see through the cottonwoods, the barns, the other outbuildings. On aching feet he literally stumbled the rest of the way to the bunkhouse, let himself in, saw startled faces, and put his forefinger across his lips.

He learned that Delira had gone to town, broken up over news of his death, which caused him to smile grimly.

"Keep it to yourselves that I'm back," he asked the men and they agreed.

After eating a hearty meal, he flopped down on his

bunk and fell asleep. The men tiptoed out, leaving him alone. He had hiked over the mountains in ranch boots with built-up heels.

In Hopeville, Jim Sloan felt buoyant as he walked with long-legged stride from the hotel over to the Trail's End where he had seen Craig Moran enter before the meeting with Delira. He found himself whistling and the world seemed good. But he was under no illusions so far as Delira was concerned. His prize had been won only because Lassiter was lying crushed at the bottom of a gorge somewhere out in the mountains. In all that territory of jumbled rocks and cross canyons, his body might never be found. And if it was, by that time the predators would have done their work and only his gleaming bones would remain.

Thinking about it made him smile. He had liked Lassiter in a way, felt sorry when he and Borling had been railroaded to prison. And yet he knew Lassiter was a rival. The same as he had known earlier that Craig Moran also stood in his way of acquiring the woman of his dreams, Delira. No matter what she might be, he loved her desperately, passionately.

And now he had an ultimatum to deliver, which caused a tingling sensation of anticipation to spread throughout his body, as he shoved a shoulder against a swing door of the Trail's End and entered. He stood just inside the door, letting it flap against his rump. His eyes took in the high ceiling with its lamps in copper shades, the sawdust strewn on the floor by a swamper that morning. The deal tables, mostly empty at this hour, the dozen or so drinkers at the bar, with bootheels hooked over the brass rail.

Moran was with Sagar and Joplin and the two other men. It was Sagar who looked around to see who had entered. He nudged Moran, who turned his head.

Jim Sloan beckoned to Sagar and Moran, taking a hitch at his belt, and sauntered over with a smile on his handsome face.

"What's on your mind, Sheriff?" Moran drawled.

"Step outside, if you will, Moran."

Moran frowned, then followed him out where they stood with their backs to the saloon wall.

"I want you to get out of the country, Moran," the sheriff said bluntly.

"Why?"

"I'll tell you just once. You're through at Muleshoe, really through this time. Don't bother Mrs. Borling again. If I hear of you giving her trouble . . ." Sloan let it hang there while he kept his eyes boring into Moran's face.

"What'll you do about it?"

"Don't push me, Moran."

"Hide behind that goddamned badge." Moran's voice was raised, attracting attention. Passers-by slowed and gaped. Some men having a discussion on the hotel veranda sat up straighter in their chairs and looked around.

"I repeat," Moran said in a nasty voice, "are you going to hide behind that goddamned badge?"

Love and the prospect of possessing a beautiful woman made Jim Sloan reckless. A feeling of exhilaration flooded through the sheriff. He actually laughed, the sound of it echoing clearly on the quiet day. Deliberately, he unpinned his badge, making a great show of it, and angled across the street. Coming up to the hotel veranda, he handed the badge to one of the men sitting stiffly in the row of chairs.

"Hold this for me, will you? For the next few minutes I am not James Sloan, sheriff, but James Sloan, private citizen."

Before he turned, he glanced in the hotel hoping for a glimpse of Delira in the lobby or perhaps coming down the stairs. But the stairs were empty and the only person in the lobby was a man going over his accounts who was leaning forward to stare at the broad smile on Jim Sloan's face.

Sloan was usually not a man given to smiling much. As he recrossed the street, he noticed the strange look on Moran's face. Was it alarm? Then Moran's features settled into an impassive mask.

"One way to get you out of town," Sloan said in ringing tones, "is to carry you in a box to the graveyard."

Moran was staring at the spot on Sloan's vest not faded by the sun where the badge was usually pinned.

At that moment, Delira, wearing a light yellow dress, came to the hotel doorway. There she froze at the sight of tense onlookers and Jim Sloan face to face with Moran over by the Trail's End. Other faces were pressed against the saloon's front windows.

Something made Jim Sloan look over his shoulder and see Delira, her hair shining in the sun, the splendid figure the yellow dress could not hide. She blew him a kiss, which instantly expanded his chest and made his heart flutter.

It produced a look of cold fury on Moran's face. Sloan, laughing, lifted his hat gallantly to Delira, replaced it on his head, then turned once again to face Moran.

Never in his life had Sloan felt more confident than he did at that moment on the boardwalk in front of the Trail's End. Twenty feet away stood Moran, his mouth twisted, his eyes murderous.

"You can see I'm no longer hiding behind my badge," Jim Sloan said. "I removed it so that in the event you should wound me . . . or even do worse . . . that it won't be held against you as it would if you were facing the sheriff. At present, I'm just an ordinary citizen. And as an ordinary citizen, I'm telling you once again to get out of Hopeville. And stay out!"

Moran had been standing stiffly, his right hand clamped to the butt of the .45 at his belt. Now he moved his hand and let it hang loosely at his side. Sloan was similarly armed, standing tall and lean, his forty-year-old-face exuding confidence.

"How is it, Moran?" Sloan's voice crackled along the street. "Do you clear out? Or . . ." He let the word fade as the growing crowd of onlookers gasped.

"You expect me to ride off and leave Muleshoe? Leave the woman I figure to marry?"

Heads swiveled from Moran to Sloan to see how he would take it.

"I see you intend it to be '*or*'. Any time, Moran. Make your play. . . ."

Moran suddenly snapped into violent action. As it

turned out, Sloan was terribly slow and knew it. This knowledge was written on his face as the first bullet struck him in the chest, his half-drawn gun at his side.

Those close to him heard Sloan cry out, "Oh, my God . . . Delira!" Already his knees were caving as the second bullet struck him in the face, diverted upward by bone and cartilage to erupt through the top of his skull. His hat was blown into the air.

He fell limply, his blood already staining the planks of the Hopeville boardwalk.

Delira had been unable to watch so had hurried to her suite and locked herself in. As she heard the gunshots, her knees began to quiver. Minutes before, Senna had returned from visiting friends in Hopeville. Delira was so sure that Sloan would be back that she ordered Senna to return to Muleshoe.

It seemed an eternity before she heard a soft knock on the door. She dashed to it, pulled the bolt and flung it open. "Jim, are you all right . . . ?"

Her voice faded into a small sound of agony. Craig Moran, wearing a faint smile of triumph, his eyes mocking, stood in the doorway.

"I killed him. There was nothing else I could do."

Desperately, she tried to close the door, but his foot was in it. Once in the room he gave her a shove that sent her stumbling backwards until she lost her balance and fell. Then he bolted the door.

"I'll scream!" she threatened, hopping to her feet.

"You do that. Everyone knows what we've been to each other. Those who don't know for sure, suspect. So it won't do you a damned bit of good to yell."

She whirled away from him, opened her mouth, her gray eyes betraying her intentions. But the scream ended in a muffled gurgle, for he had whipped a bandanna from his pocket and wrapped it across her mouth. This he knotted at the back of her head. Then, as she tried frantically to undo the knot, he removed his belt and used it to fasten her hands behind her back.

Then he picked her up and flung her down on the bed. Leisurely, he removed her yellow dress and where it caught on her bound wrists, he tore it apart. Likewise with her camisole.

"By the way, I used the power of Muleshoe to convince those fools out there to appoint Meager Joplin sheriff until an election can be held," Moran said with a smile. "So if you've got any idea of running to the law, forget it."

She thrashed about on the bed, with muffled sounds of rage coming from behind the gag in her mouth.

"The start of our honeymoon," he said with a laugh. "So enjoy it."

When he was finished with her he unfastened her wrists and removed the gag. She lay on the bed, panting, hating him.

"I'll tell everybody what you did to me," she threatened.

"They won't believe you."

She snatched up the yellow dress. "They'll believe this!"

"I'll say you tore it yourself. To make me look bad." He went to the door, then looked back at her. "I'm going over to the Trail's End to toast our new sheriff. But we'll leave for the ranch within the hour. Be ready."

Then he went out. Of all times, she hadn't had Senna's protection. Had she been here, though, Delira supposed, Moran would simply have frightened her into leaving.

What she needed now were her Muleshoe men. She was confident they'd rally around her. That she had ignored most of them, snubbed the few who came near her, never entered her steaming mind. All she wanted was to get to Muleshoe and the protection of her crew. Then let Moran try something!

Still fuming, she wadded up the torn yellow dress, shoved it into the armoire, got a blue one and dropped it over her head. Hoping that Senna might have delayed her departure, she hurried along the street toward the livery barn, not looking at the knots of men along the walk discussing the death of Jim Sloan. His body had been carried to the undertaker's behind the furniture store.

Fresh drops of blood on the walk made her wonder vaguely if it was Sloan's. But she didn't dwell on it. Her prime objective now was to bring Craig Moran to his knees. She herself could cheerfully strip the skin from his living flesh.

"You hear 'bout the sheriff gettin' killed, Mrs. Borling?"

The voice came at her from the shadowed interior of the big stable. "Is Mrs. Senna here yet?" she demanded imperiously.

"No, ma'am, she done left for Muleshoe."

"But it was only a few minutes ago."

"I'm sorry, ma'am, but—"

"I want to rent a horse. Quickly, please!"

The lanky hostler, chewing on a length of straw, materialized from the shadows. He was rubbing the side of his face in perplexity. "Reckon I ain't got no horse to rent but Big Red, ma'am. If you wait till Mr. Danvers gets back, maybe he'll rent you—"

"Put a saddle on this Big Red. *Now!*"

"Yes, Ma'am." And he loped off into deeper shadows, then led out a big red roan. The hostler looked dubiously at her long skirts and said, "Just happened to think. We ain't got no side saddle, Mrs. Borling."

"Never mind. Give me a hand!"

He made a step of his two hands and boosted her into the saddle. As her skirts were pulled up her stockinged legs, he tried not to look. He stood riveted as she lashed the big horse with the ends of the reins and it bolted out the wide doorway in a dead run.

When Milt Danvers, a chubby, cigar-chomping little man, returned from discussing the shootout at the Trail's End, he found his hostler fretting. It was then the hostler unburdened himself.

"Holy Christ!" Danvers exclaimed. "You hadn't oughta rented her Big Red!"

"I was scared not to."

"I don't know whether she can even ride. All I've ever seen her in is the ranch buggy."

"She went outta here lickety-split, hangin' on."

"Well, let's hope she can set a saddle proper." Danvers gave a shake of his head.

\* \* \*

A mile west of town, Delira finally tried bringing Big Red down to a slower pace because the jouncing about was killing her. But the harder she pulled on the reins, the faster the big horse seemed to run. Panicked, she felt her seat in the saddle begin to slip. As she pulled frantically on the reins, the speeding horse left the road and cut across the rocky open country.

On this uneven terrain the ride became even worse and she lost her left stirrup. When she tried desperately to find it again with her pawing foot, she lost her balance.

A strangled cry burst from her lips as she fell, her right foot still anchored in its stirrup. Some of her panic had spread to the horse, intensified because of the dragging weight over the rocky ground. Her screams ended abruptly but still the horse continued its erratic run, gradually slowing and then coming to a full stop. There was blood in the lather at its muzzle from the sawing on the bit. But it was nothing compared to the blood that soiled the lifeless form of Delira, her foot still twisted securely in the stirrup.

Moran had seen her erratic flight from town through a window of the Trail's End. At first, he was amused as he thought about it, then be became concerned. Was she spurring that big horse or was he running away with her?

He made up his mind suddenly and caught up his own mount at the hitching post and went after her. Finally, he saw Big Red standing with head down, anchored by a weight midway across a rock-strewn clearing. Even at this distance he sized up the situation accurately.

Because he didn't want the tracks of his horse to be found near her body, he decided not to go for a closer look. Hearing a rider coming from the direction of town, he ducked into some cottonwoods nearby. The rider was Milt Danvers of the Hopeville Livery Stable. Danvers, at a lope, rode right on past without noticing Big Red and the rest of it.

When Danvers was out of sight, Moran turned back quickly for Hopeville and spurred his horse into a dead run. Plans flashed through his mind as he rode furiously and he finally seized on one.

# Chapter Twenty-two

Milt Danvers rode all the way out to Muleshoe to make sure Mrs. Borling had arrived safely. There he received a double shock. The first being that she had never arrived, the second was seeing Lassiter in the flesh, not dead as everyone had supposed.

"We'll go look for her," Lassiter announced.

She was found shortly before sundown. "Oh, my *God!*" Lassiter cried, upon dismounting. "Nobody deserves to die like that."

She was taken to Hopeville and placed next to Jim Sloan in the lean-to behind the furniture store, united with him at least in death.

While searching for Delira, Lassiter had been filled in concerning the death of Jim Sloan. When he arrived in town he wasn't too surprised to see the giant Joplin come swaggering up, with Sloan's star pinned to his shirt.

Behind him were Moran and several curious townspeople. Lassiter had finished his business with the bald undertaker and was just about to leave the lean-to.

"Heard about Mrs. Borling," Joplin said in his heavy voice, his yellowish eyes drilling into Lassiter's face. "Thought you oughta know that just before she left town, she signed over Muleshoe to the fella she figured to marry with tomorrow—Craig Moran."

"You are a damned liar," Lassiter said through his teeth and the onlookers, all except Moran, began to break for cover.

A hissing lantern gave off enough light in the lean-to so that Lassiter could read the paper Joplin was thrusting into his face. It was a quit-claim deed in a woman's hand. It was signed Delira Borling.

"That isn't her signature," Lassiter charged, taking a chance that it wasn't.

"She was upset when she wrote it, the sheriff nearly killin' her betrothed. So maybe it don't look quite right, but she signed it. And there were witnesses."

Lassiter saw the names—Moran and Sagar.

He looked over at the lump on the shelf next to Jim Sloan, wrapped in a blood-stained blanket. Her coffin would not be open at the funeral because of the condition of her face that the rocky ground had destroyed.

Again Joplin thrust the alleged quit-claim deed under Lassiter's nose. Lassiter brushed it aside. "It's a forgery," he said bluntly, which caused those crowding to exchange glances.

"Here's a letter she wrote to Craig Moran," Joplin persisted, for the benefit of the onlookers, no doubt. "Wrote it here in town when she thought you was dead. Tellin' him how glad she was that you wouldn't be around to bother her no more an' beggin' Moran to come back to Muleshoe. It's the same handwriting as on the quit-claim deed."

Instead of flying into a rage as everyone expected, Lassiter turned his back and stalked out.

"He's upset, you can see that," Moran said to the growing crowd. He jerked his head at Joplin and the two of them left the lean-to.

Everything was going well so far, Moran believed. As near as he could tell, the majority of those crowded around the entrance of the lean-to had believed the story of the quit-claim deed and the letter. The letter had been an afterthought, an inspiration really.

When Moran arrived back in town after seeing Delira's body, her right foot still trapped in the stirrup of Big Red, he had kept to back alleys until reaching a side door of the Full House. He slipped inside and signaled to Doxie who was talking to her bartender.

Because Moran was a good customer she listened to what he had to say. As he talked, a frown materialized on her rouged face, under the mass of hennaed hair. She toyed with numerous necklaces draped around her plump neck.

"What'll Lassiter say about this?" she asked when he had finished.

"Lassiter's dead as last Christmas."

"I ain't never met him, but I know his rep. I wouldn't wanta tangle with that son."

"No chance of that."

"You sure I won't get in no trouble over this?" she asked, watching his face.

"Joplin's sheriff. How could there be trouble?"

"All right," she said with a shrug of heavy shoulders. "Come on in the office. I got pen an' ink there."

After she wrote out the quit-claim deed according to his instructions, it popped into his head about the letter.

"Just in case somebody wants to compare her handwriting," Moran said with a tight grin.

When the letter was written he sprinkled dirt on it and folded and refolded it many times as if he had been carrying it in his pocket for a time.

"You ain't been in lately," Doxie said in her small, cluttered office. "Some of my gals was askin' about you."

"Tell 'em not to worry. Once I get things settled, they'll see me plenty."

That was several hours ago. So far, Moran was well satisfied with the result. When he'd had Doxie write out the quit-claim deed and the letter he'd believed Lassiter to be lying dead at the bottom of one of the deep canyons west of Muleshoe. To have seen him riding into town— alive—with Delira's body had been a shock. But in the dangerous games he had been playing, one thing he had learned was resilience. He had quickly recovered.

After leaving the lean-to, Lassiter entered the hotel by the rear door and went directly to Ellen Stencoe's room. But there was no response to his repeated knocking. He quickly went to the lobby and asked the clerk if he knew where she had gone.

The clerk, his hair slicked back with pomade, looked up from a ledger he was working on under lamplight. "Checked out, she did," he announced.

"Where'd she go?"

"I wasn't on duty when she left. Ed was. So all I know is that she ain't here no more."

Disappointed, Lassiter stepped onto the veranda and halted there to figure his next move. He hadn't counted on Ellen checking out, but under the circumstances he supposed it had been inevitable. But he was let down because of plans he had made.

Stars made a blazing pattern of silver across the sky in competition to a rising moon just edging over the mountains. Coyotes had begun yelping north of town, and from the direction of the livery barn a restless mule began to bray.

He was about to leave the hotel doorway when something made him glance to his right. A figure was huddled in one of the chairs under the veranda overhang at the far end.

"Ellen," he called softly, noting the stiff way she sat in the chair, staring at him. She wore a cloak against the evening chill. At her feet were a portmanteau and a carpetbag.

"You checked out without telling me," he said as he approached her.

"The stage is late or I'd have been gone hours ago."

Because there seemed to be hurt as well as anger in her voice he couldn't quite judge her mood. Hooking one of the chairs with his foot, he drew it closer and sat down. "I'm glad I found you. I've got something to talk over. . . ."

"First, let me say that I'm terribly sorry about Mrs. Borling. It must have been terrible to find her like that."

"It wasn't one of life's more rewarding experiences, no."

"And you miss her terribly. . . ."

"I'm sorry she's dead. I can say that about most anyone." His reservations on the subject were locked around the images of Moran, Joplin, and Sagar. "Where's Ralph?"

"What difference does that make?"

"Because he's part of what I want to talk about."

"There's nothing to discuss, Lassiter. Nothing at all."

"Look, that night . . . I'm sorry about it. I shouldn't have . . . taken advantage of you. And I did and I'm sorry."

"No one takes advantage of me." She sat up straight in the chair, her jaw set. "What I did was because I wanted it." Her voice broke.

"Tell me where Ralph is."

"He won't want to see me. And I certainly don't want to see him." She put a hand to her eyes and squeezed them shut.

"What did you quarrel about?"

"You mainly. Because of that . . . that stupid letter I wrote him saying I was in love. . . ."

He reached out and gripped her hand. "Listen to me . . ."

But the words kept spilling out of her, bordering on hysteria. "He wanted me to return to Tucson with him. He thinks he can get his old job back. . . ."

"Ellen . . ."

"I wrote my married sister the same kind of letter I wrote Ralph, telling her about . . . about you. And now it's all over Tucson."

"What of it? If you married Ralph, people would forget it."

"I'm not going back. I have a little money . . . money put aside for the ranch Ralph always wanted to buy. I . . . I'm going to make a new life for myself out in San Francisco."

That was when he began talking earnestly about his proposition that had come to him so clearly during the ride back to town with Delira's body. Ellen and Ralph Benson to marry and operate Muleshoe and raise Rance Borling.

"The kid likes you very much, Ellen. He's told me. In fact, outside of myself . . . and I may be bragging a little there . . . you're the best friend he's ever had."

"Oh, I don't know, Lassiter."

"Give the boy a home. And with it should go a half interest in Muleshoe. Without you, the boy would have nothing. He has no relatives, nobody."

Some men came out of the Trail's End down the block, the swinging doors throwing a streak of lamplight into the street. Their boots echoed hollowly on the board-walk as they went to their horses and started riding away.

Lassiter persisted. "We'll get the lawyer to make it all legal. You'll be guardians of Rance and . . ."

She looked at him out of large gray eyes and said, "Why don't you stay here and do it?"

"It's not my nature to stay in one place too long."

This caused a little laugh to break from her lips. "If I'd only known that. What a fool I've been."

He gripped her hand. "No fool at all. Just a human being. We gave something to each other that night."

"Your proposition sounds wonderful, but it's too late."

"If Ralph has left town, tell me which way he went and I'll go after him."

"We were talking just before you came out of the hotel. Talking . . . arguing. He said something about going to that *place* at the far end of town."

"You mean the Full House?"

"Where they have the girls." Her voice was strained.

"You wait here. Get your room back. Promise me, Ellen. This could be the most important decision of our lives."

She studied him a moment, moonlight touching her pretty face, her even white teeth sunk into her lower lip. "I . . . I promise."

At a lope, Lassiter headed for the eastern end of Hopeville. He paused outside the door of a squat building, surrounded by trees, to get his breath. Then he pushed his way into the smoky interior. There were some dozen or more patrons either lined up at the short bar or sharing tables with girls. He found Ralph Benson occupying a table against the wall. He was just pouring a drink from a bottle. A blond girl in a black dress split to her knees was sitting on his lap.

"Go find somebody else," Lassiter told the girl and sat down at the table.

The girl hopped to her feet and yelled, "Doxie!"

Everyone looked around. The place became very still.

Ralph Benson had some difficulty focusing his eyes. "You got some nerve buttin' in, Lassiter."

A tall, buxom woman with hennaed hair came thumping across the room, her necklaces swinging from a ponderous neck just in time to hear the last.

"You Lassiter?" she demanded.

"Yeah."

"I heard you was dead."

"Not very. I'm taking Benson out of here. Any objections?"

"Jeezus, no, not to you. If I'd known you was still alive I'd never have . . ." She closed her mouth until it became two red creases across her round face.

"You'd never have done what?" Lassiter asked softly, but she was hurrying away.

"You'll play hell gettin' me to leave here," Ralph Benson said thickly. "Here I'm appreciated. . . ." He stumbled over the word and finally got it straight.

He was reaching clumsily for his gun, those nearby whirling to get out of the way, when Lassiter hit him a solid blow on the jaw. Benson would have struck the table with his chin had not Lassiter grabbed him. He stuck the man's gun in his own belt, then slung him over his shoulder. He took a look around the smoky room at the staring eyes and moved to the door. Doxie appeared from behind a partition and opened it for him.

"I only seen you from a distance, Lassiter, but you're welcome any time. . . ."

Out in the street, Lassiter slapped Benson awake.

Two men dismounted at the rack, saw what was going on and laughed. One of them said, "It'll take me to midnight to get that drunk." They both went inside. The door closed, shutting off the beam of lamplight.

When Lassiter finally got Benson on his feet and walking he talked earnestly. "You've hurt Ellen."

"You done a little hurting yourself, Lassiter."

"I know and I apologized." Thinking that was enough to say on the subject, he outlined it all just as he had done for Ellen Stencoe, but Benson was more receptive.

"The chance of a lifetime," he said in awe. He was rubbing his jaw where Lassiter had struck him. He paused in a shaft of moonlight through trees that bordered the dark street and looked up into Lassiter's face. "Are you sure Ellen wants to do it?"

Lassiter nodded. Then he thought he might as well try to clear up the rest of it . . . to a point. "Ellen thought from some of the things I said that I was going to marry her, I guess. That's all there was to it. She was away from home and lonely and her brother had just been killed." He spread his hands.

"That all there was between you two?" Benson looked him straight in the eye.

"That's all there was, so help me." From experience, Lassiter had learned that sometimes a lie saves unnecessary pain and heartache.

Benson stood there, thinking that over while Lassiter filled him in about Moran and the fake quit-claim deed.

"What do you aim to do about Moran?" Benson wanted to know. He was rubbing his sore jaw again.

"Tomorrow you and Ellen get married. We'll have the lawyer draw up the papers."

"Then what?"

"I'm going after Moran."

"I'll help."

Lassiter shook his head. "You stay out of it."

"Think I'm gonna let you do it alone?"

"I don't figure to see Ellen a widow the first week she's married." He hurried away, having things to do, and not wishing to argue further with Benson that night.

# Chapter Twenty-three

Lassiter went to see the boy, knowing it might very well be the last time. Doctor Steenbolt, busy by lamplight, gave him a nod. He took Rance outside and told him of the new arrangement. Rance was delighted that Ellen Stencoe would be part of his new family. But when he mentioned Ralph Benson's part in it, the boy's face fell.

"But you're gonna marry her, ain't you, Lassiter?"

"Ain't's not a good word for you, Rance. Ellen would be disappointed."

"Answer me, Lassiter. Ain't . . . aren't you gonna marry her?"

Lassiter shook his head and explained the new arrangement more fully.

"But why don't you marry her?" Rance asked, wide-eyed in the moonlight that filtered through trees beside the doctor's establishment.

"People marry for love, Rance. And we don't love each other."

When Rance seemed crestfallen, Lassiter quickly

said, "Ralph Benson is a fine man. He's the kind of man your pa would want to raise you."

"But what about you, Lassiter?" the boy wailed.

"I've got things to do. Places to go."

"Take me with you."

Lassiter shook his head. "But one of these days I'll be coming back to see you."

That seemed to mollify the boy somewhat. He walked Rance to his quarters, then called Steenbolt away from his patient. He had just set the arm of a saddlebum named Reamer.

"What is it, Lassiter?" Steenbolt could still not quite rid his voice of animosity. In the lamplight the doctor's bearded face seemed tense.

"I'd like you to keep an eye on Rance."

"It's what I have been doing," was the sharp reply.

"There's nobody I can turn to. Sloan's dead and our new sheriff . . ." Lassiter gave a dry laugh. "The hell with him. I'm afraid somebody might make a try for the boy. Have you got a weapon?"

"A .45 that I know how to use. Just who do you think might harm the boy?"

"Moran."

"I realize he's done some underhanded things but I doubt if such a charming gentleman would harm a boy."

"How do you think he got his broken leg?"

"He was lost in the mountains and fell."

Lassiter gave a sound of disgust. "Just keep your eyes open, will you?"

"Lassiter, I can protect the boy as well as myself." They locked eyes and then the doctor said, "I'm sorry, Lassiter. I'm out of sorts tonight. I lost a patient today."

Lassiter gave him a squeeze on the arm. "I can understand. My hunch is that Moran will come to town for Mrs. Borling's funeral tomorrow. Just keep your eyes open. It's all I ask."

"What'll you be doing, Lassiter?"

"Settling old scores."

Rance was standing in the doorway to his room, a look of sadness on his small face. When Lassiter lifted a hand to him, the boy said, "Will I see you again, Lassiter?"

"Sure you will." Lassiter wore a wide grin as he stepped from the house. But once outside it faded quickly. Three horsemen were just pulling up in front of the Steenbolt quarters.

It was Ellick, Delaney and Hopkins. Ellick dismounted and came over, his face grave in the light spilling from the windows.

"Benson said you were over here," Ellick began.

"What're you three doing in town?"

"Moran's taken over out at Muleshoe. He said Mrs. Borling's dead an' you figured to quit the country."

"Not quite. The rest of the boys with you?"

Ellick shook his head. "Only us is left. The rest of the outfit headed north. Somethin' was said about Denver."

Lassiter felt let down that his men had quit on him.

"Moran said somethin' about possession bein' nine points of the law," Ellick said.

"Possession, but not for long. Are you game to help throw him off?"

Ellick dug his toe in the dirt and seemed ill at ease. "I'll have to put it to you straight, Lassiter. We was

231

gonna ride wherever you figured to go . . . if you wanted us. But only so long as it was out of this part of the territory."

"I see." Lassiter's voice was cold.

"I'm sorry, Lassiter, but we figure you got no chance. There's eight of 'em out there an' only four of us, countin' you."

"It's your decision, Ellick."

"Dammit, Lassiter . . ."

"Go on, get going. Seems I've got some hiring to do."

Wheeling, he stalked off in the direction of the hotel he could see through the trees. Ellick called out something but Lassiter did not turn around.

He knew that sometime during the funeral or shortly afterward he and Moran would have to face up. And only one of them would come out of it alive.

At the hotel he signed for a room. The startled clerk ran a hand over his pomaded hair and didn't open his mouth. The dark look on Lassiter's face was frightening.

He still had not fully recovered from his long and painful hike out of the mountains, and he fell asleep at once. He came awake sometime later by a light tapping on his door, sounding like the touch of a woman. Ellen was the one that sprang into his mind. Swearing under his breath, he started for the door. But something made him go back for the gun he had placed on the floor beside his bed.

The tapping sound came again. "Who is it?" Lassiter called through the door.

"Joe Sellers, the night clerk . . ."

Something in the clerk's voice, sounding of doom, made Lassiter feel as if a bucket of ice water had been thrown in his face. He unlocked the door and flung it open. "What is it?" Lassiter demanded.

Under the pomaded hair the clerk's face was sweaty and pale as death. Sellers placed a finger across his trembling lips and crowded into the room. He closed the door and leaned against it, visibly shaking.

"Miss Stencoe," he began hoarsely, "is why I'm here. . . ."

"What about her?" Lassiter cried, and again Sellers placed a finger across his lips, indicating silence.

"There were two of them. Masked. They came in the back door, marched me down the hall. There was Miss Stencoe. She was gagged and . . . and I suspect, tied. Although I couldn't be sure."

"Go on, tell me the rest," Lassiter urged in a whisper.

"They had evidently let her put on a cloak over her night dress."

"Never mind that. What did they say?"

"They . . . they told me to get you. I wasn't to say a word to anyone else, or Miss Stencoe would . . . would die. You're to ride out the Muleshoe road . . . alone . . . if you ever want to see her alive again."

Lassiter felt as if kicked in the stomach. "Is that all they said? Nothing else?"

"That's all. I . . . I was half asleep . . . about ready to close up when one of them rammed a gun in my ribs."

Lassiter was buckling on his gun. His face was ashen.

"Do as they said, Sellers. Don't talk to *anybody* about this."

"I . . . I won't."

Numbly, Lassiter hurried through the deserted hotel

lobby and out into the night. There was still a light on at the Trail's End on the corner, but the rest of the town seemed deserted. From the position of the full moon overhead, he judged it to be about midnight.

He ran to the livery barn, his boots crunching in the gravel. He was halfway through saddling his horse when the night hostler woke up. The gaunt man rubbed his eyes and sat up on his cot.

"You're ridin' late, Lassiter."

"Yep."

A second figure appeared from the rear of the big barn from the shadows. It was Ralph Benson, looking half awake and brushing bits of straw from his clothing.

"I heard your name mentioned, Lassiter. What's up?"

"What're you doing here?" he demanded as he prepared to mount, but Benson grabbed him by an arm.

"I gave the hostler a dollar for a bed," Benson said through his teeth, staring at Lassiter by the dim glow of a night lantern. "What're you doing here is what I'm interested in!"

"Let go of my arm, Benson."

"Have you seen Ellen?"

Lassiter's mind was spinning by then and he started to speak, the words tumbling out of him. "She's been—" Then he broke off. "No, I haven't seen her."

"Liar! I can tell by your voice."

"I don't want to have to pop you on the jaw twice in the same night, Benson!"

"You won't get a chance."

Releasing his hold on Lassiter's arm, he spun away and seized a rifle resting on pegs above the night hostler's cot. The hostler gave a squeak of fear and rolled off the cot to his knees.

Before Benson could work the loading lever, Lassiter lunged, tore the rifle out of his hands and struck him a solid blow on the point of the chin with the barrel. Benson collapsed, spreading his length across the straw-littered runway.

By then, Lassiter was in the saddle and spurring out the wide doorway into the moon-swept night. A cooling breeze struck his face as he slowed the horse to a walk so as not to call attention to himself.

If all went well, Lassiter doubted that Moran would kill Ellen. It was Lassiter he wanted.

One thing he had to say for Moran. He knew how to bait a trap.

# Chapter Twenty-four

Ellick, just returning from the privy behind the Trail's End, saw the lone horseman ride past the building and continue along the west road. Here the moonlight was strong, almost as bright as noon, and he could clearly see that it was Lassiter, riding in the direction of Muleshoe. Instantly a wave of shame broke over him and he hurried inside.

Delaney was slouched at the bar, singing softly under his breath. The emaciated Jack Hopkins was pouring himself another drink, slopping the whiskey because of a trembling hand.

Ellick, his mind clearing of whiskey fumes, seized Hopkins by the wrist. "Know what I just seen?"

"A ghost." Hopkins tittered and fell against the bar.

"Lassiter. He's headin' for Muleshoe. An' he's *alone*."

He looked meaningfully at Hopkins and at Delaney, who had stopped singing and lifted his head to stare at Ellick.

"You mean he's gonna face up to Moran with nobody to side him?" Delaney said thickly.

"Dammit, we can't let him do that," Ellick said. "We was wrong to even let him try."

"S'pose so . . ." Hopkins muttered and put his head on the bar.

"We're guilty of turnin' our backs on him," Ellick continued. "That's why we've been here tryin' to drown it in forty rod."

The few other patrons were watching them, a trio of avenging drunks now staggering for the doors. Hopkins didn't make it. He staggered over to an empty deal table, collapsed in a chair and began to snore. Ellick and Delaney were at a stumbling run for their horses. The cooling night breeze in their faces had a reasonably sobering effect as they headed westward out of Hopeville, which would eventually take them to the Muleshoe road.

Lassiter heard the sounds of riders and reined in, a scowl on his dark face. Drawing his gun, he waited, not knowing what to expect because the riders were coming from Hopeville at a gallop. Around a bend in the road, sheltered by tall trees, he saw the two shadowy horsemen and lifted his gun. Where the trees thinned and moonlight spread he recognized them.

"Ellick, what the hell!" he growled as the riders reined in to stare at Lassiter whose horse was broadside in the road.

"Seen you head this way an' figured we was wrong not to be sidin' you. . . ."

"Get back to town. Both of you!"

"Hey, that ain't right," Ellick sputtered.

"You heard me, goddamnit!"

"You gotta tell us why," Ellick insisted.

"Because . . . because you're both drunk and can do me no good."

"By the time we get to Muleshoe we'll be stone sober."

"Look, I'm asking you. Go back to Hopeville."

"But you ain't told us no good reason."

Lassiter's hand was suddenly moist on the grip of the .44. He holstered the weapon. "I can't tell you why I want you to go back to town."

"Moran's got some hold on you, sure as Christ!" Ellick guessed.

"That he has," Lassiter admitted in his frustration. "But I can't talk about it. I'm under orders not to! Can't you get that through your thick skulls?"

Ellick drew himself up in the saddle and gave Delaney a slight of the head, who was starting to splutter, "Whatever you say, boss," Ellick said to a rigid Lassiter.

Lassiter's voice shook as he said, "Don't try and sneak after me."

"Wasn't thinkin' of that at all," Ellick said.

"There's another life at stake in this. And it isn't mine."

That produced a moment of silence. Through the trees a pair of yellow eyes could be seen, possibly a prowling bobcat.

Ellick cleared his throat. "We'll be headin' back, Lassiter."

"Can I depend on it?"

"Yeah."

"Don't try and fool me. It's too important. When you . . . realize who else is mixed up in this, you'll understand."

"You told us an' we listened an' now we're a-goin'."

Ellick was first to turn his horse and start back. After a moment, Delaney followed him.

Tensely, Lassiter listened to the sounds of their mounts after they had disappeared around the bend in the road. By straining his ears, he could still hear them for quite a while. Only then did he blow out his breath and let down slightly. It had warmed him that two of his men, at least, had had second thoughts about deserting him, even if it might have taken frontier whiskey to spur their consciences.

Lassiter started riding again, the breath tight in his lungs, knowing it could happen at any time. The instructions of the abductors, relayed by the night clerk, had been to ride out the Muleshoe road. Not necessarily to Muleshoe itself—just the road, which he had been on for a quarter of a mile after it branched off from the main road.

Suddenly, two horsemen angled in from either side of the road ahead. They both held rifles centered on his breastbone.

"Hold it, Lassiter." It was Petey Sagar.

And the other man was the black-bearded Sam Dirk.

"Where's the girl?" Lassiter demanded.

"You'll see. Step down." Sagar gestured with his rifle.

Gingerly, Lassiter dismounted. "Throw your gun on the ground," was Sam Dirk's order.

Under the circumstances, with Ellen's life hanging in the balance, there was nothing else for Lassiter to do. In a moment his .44 lay gleaming on the road in the moonlight.

"Over here," Sagar ordered and jerked his head toward a creek that flowed across the road and vanished into some trees on the south side. Although shadows were deeper under the trees, there was still enough moonlight so that Lassiter could make out Moran squatted beside the creek.

"Ambush for Lassiter," Moran said with a nasty chuckle. He was holding two bandannas in the waters of the swiftly flowing creek.

"Where's Ellen Stencoe?" Lassiter demanded.

"I don't have to tell you, but for the hell of it I will. She's at Muleshoe."

"Have you harmed her?"

"She's safe enough . . . for now."

"You'll never get away with this, Moran. You'll hang."

"You're bluffing. You know damn well you are."

At that moment, Joplin stepped from the brush, a rifle under his arm, grinning broadly. "Damn if it ain't Lassiter," he said with a harsh laugh.

Moran finally got to his feet, holding the two dripping bandannas. Then he began to leisurely wind one around the knuckles of his left hand. The other one was wound around his right.

"I figure to keep the Stencoe gal alive . . . if all goes well," Moran said meaningfully. "Now about the boy . . ." Moran, grinning, let his words fade in the night.

"What about the boy?" Lassiter cried, jumping at the bait.

"I'll raise him. Oh, I'll get me a woman eventually who can help. By the time he's fourteen or fifteen he'll be my man. Maybe the quit-claim deed won't stand up in court. But the kid's claim will. So either way I'll control Muleshoe."

Lassiter's mind was numbed. What Moran intended to do with his hands wrapped in the wet bandannas was evident. But Moran told him anyway.

"You've cost me, Lassiter. Cost me plenty. I figure to cut you to pieces first. Before I put a bullet in your goddamn hide."

"How'll you explain my murder?"

"It won't be murder. We shot it out fair and square. With our estimable sheriff as witness."

"You say you're going to cut me up first. So how'll you explain the way I look?"

"We shot it out at the edge of a cliff. There's one not far from here. This time your body will be found at the bottom. Pretty well smashed up. You'll be one big mess. The marks I put on you now won't show."

"I see."

"Get your fists up, Lassiter. I'm coming after you."

At least Moran seemed to be giving him a chance. For what reason, Lassiter couldn't imagine. But it was enough that he had these few precious minutes.

Hoping to get in the first punch, Lassiter lunged, aiming at Moran's grin, hoping to smash it from his face. But after the first step, something caught his ankles, and as he began to fall, he saw that Sam Dirk had squatted and tripped him with the barrel of his rifle.

As he fell, Lassiter felt a booming smash to his forehead, and another to his left cheekbone. He fell and rolled aside, despite the thunder in his head, and managed to escape Moran's boots.

Dizzy from the twin blows, Lassiter staggered to his feet, but Moran hit him a glancing blow along the jaw that peeled the skin.

Blood from the trio of lacerations spilled down Lassiter's face and began to soak into his clothing. Sagar, Dirk and Joplin were yelling encouragement to Moran, who sprang and knocked Lassiter to the ground.

"On your feet, Lassiter," Moran challenged, standing over him. "Or shall I kick your brains into the dust?"

Lassiter was barely able to squirm aside as Moran's right boot whistled past his face.

Feigning weakness, he suddenly half stood and lurched toward Joplin, who threw up his thick arm to fend him off. But quick as the head of a striking snake, Lassiter's right hand darted for Joplin's gun belt. Too late, Joplin tried to bring his rifle into firing position as Lassiter laid the whole frame of the big .45 diagonally across his face. Joplin's nose, which had been broken in their previous fight in the wagon yard, was violently smashed again.

As Joplin, with a low groan, spread his bulk across the damp bank of the creek, Lassiter stepped back, gripping the .45.

"Make a move and you're dead," he threatened Sagar and Dirk, also intending the warning to be for Moran. But Moran had ducked into shadows where the trees grew thicker down the creek.

Before Lassiter could open his mouth, Moran reappeared. His tight grin barely showed above one of Ellen Stencoe's shoulders. Her eyes, wide with fright, were riveted on Lassiter. Her dark hair was loose about her face, brushing the collar of a brown traveling cloak. She was gagged and her wrists were evidently bound behind her.

"My ace in the hole," Moran said, still grinning. "I toyed with you, Lassiter. I wanted you to think you were about to win, then slam the door in your face. Throw down the gun or she . . ."

Moran didn't need to elaborate because Lassiter could see the muzzle of a weapon pressing against Ellen Stencoe's right ear.

"I figured the old Lassiter luck might come shining through," Moran went on. "So I was prepared. *Drop the gun, I said!*"

In that fraction of time, Lassiter, his face smeared with blood, weighed his chances of striking the small target of Moran's face that barely showed above Ellen's shoulder. Or maybe he could shoot him in the legs before Moran could fire a bullet into the girl's skull.

Lassiter knew he had lost, so he relaxed his grip on the weapon, starting to let it fall. It was then that Ellen gave a sudden mighty twist of her body that broke Moran's hold. Moran swore and started to follow Ellen's drop to the ground by altering his aim with the gun. But at the last instant he remembered Lassiter and brought up the weapon. Both guns exploded at once, Moran's throwing a streak of fire skyward, Lassiter's aimed at Moran's broad chest.

There was yelling as Moran took a staggering step, and the sound of horses.

"Hold it!" the harsh command sounding like Ellick.

Lassiter was already spinning. All he could hope for was to get one of them—Sagar. Sam Dirk was out of reach. Sagar's shot whistled past Lassiter's bloodied cheek and into a tree trunk. When Lassiter dropped the hammer, he was gratified to see Sagar leap into the air, his head back, and start to collapse. Lassiter braced himself for Dirk's bullet, but instead there was the crack of a rifle. Lassiter turned in time to see Sam Dirk fold at the middle and fall to the ground. Sagar was already down, moaning.

"I got the black-bearded bastard!" It was Ralph Benson, bare-headed, gripping a rifle, appearing at Ellick's side.

Lassiter was rushing to Ellen. "Somebody gimme a knife!" Then he remembered Joplin's boot and reached over to the unconscious man and withdrew a Bowie knife. He cut Ellen free and removed the gag.

She was in Lassiter's arms, sobbing. "I was so frightened. . . ."

"You were brave. The bravest!"

Then he pushed the weeping girl in Ralph Benson's direction. A recovering Ellen sagged against Benson's chest and he held her closely. She looked up worriedly at a deep gash on the point of his chin, where Lassiter had struck him with a rifle barrel.

"What happened?" she asked in a weak voice.

"Stumbled when I ran for my horse." His eyes sought Lassiter's.

"How'd you come to get in on this mess?" Lassiter asked when he caught his breath.

Benson said that when he came to in the stable, he recalled that Lassiter had acted strangely when questioned about Ellen. This caused Benson to rush to the hotel where he found Ellen missing. A stunned night clerk babbled the rest of it. He had overtaken Ellick and Delaney on the Muleshoe road.

"I was damn lucky to get in that shot," he finished.

Lassiter turned to Ellick and Delaney and said, "One thing for sure, I'll put in a good word for you with your new bosses, Rance Borling and Ralph Benson. And, of course, Ellen Stencoe who'll be Mrs. Benson by then."

Lassiter then unpinned the sheriff's badge from Joplin's shirt, and dropped it into his pocket. Then he got the big man on his feet. He was moaning, as was Petey Sagar. After loading the bodies of Moran and Dirk across the back of one of the horses, they started back for Hopeville.

"What you aim to do with us?" Joplin said nasally because of his smashed nose.

"Kidnapping."

"I never done it. It was Sagar an' Dirk who done it."

"You were in on it. I wonder how you'll make out down at Rimshaw as a prisoner instead of captain of the guards."

Joplin shuddered but said nothing.

There was little to choose between the condition of his face and Lassiter's. Before mounting one of the spare horses, Ellen gingerly touched the cuts and abrasions on Lassiter made by the wet bandannas wrapped around Moran's fists.

"A terrible thing Moran did to you," she whispered.

"He did worse to you." He gave her arm a squeeze and let Benson help her into the saddle.

In town, Lassiter woke up the undertaker, got Jim Sloan's keys from the man and locked Sagar and

Joplin in the town jail. Ellen went to the hotel to try and get her nerves unstrung.

Then he went down to get Steenbolt to take care of Sagar's wound.

"More of your handiwork, Lassiter," Steenbolt said soberly, then his stiffened lips gave way to a smile. "Thank God you survived."

After Sagar was cared for, Steenbolt went to work on Lassiter's face.

In the morning, there was a wedding to attend, the service performed by the Reverend Scott Lynde. Lassiter and a happy Rance Borling were witnesses along with most of the townspeople, who crowded the small church and overflowed into the yard.

When it came time for Lassiter to kiss the bride, Ellen whispered, "I'll never forget you. And thanks for everything you've done for us . . . Ralph and me."

One day just before winter, Rance Borling came rushing into the big house at Muleshoe from the foreman's quarters that Lassiter had been occupying.

"Lassiter's *gone!*" he cried in a stricken voice.

And when this was confirmed by Ellen, she put her arms around him and said, "One day he'll come riding back. You'll see."

"I miss him already."

Ellen made no reply, but when the boy looked away, she wiped her eyes and went to report the sad news to her husband.

# SONS OF THUNDER
# COTTON SMITH

No one in the small Texas town of Clark Springs knows that their minister's real name is Rule Cordell, or that he used to be one of the most notorious outlaws the Confederacy had ever seen. He's been trying very hard to put his days as a pistol-fighter behind him, but that's getting harder to do lately. When his friends and neighbors are threatened with losing their family spreads to a cunning carpetbagger, Rule realizes it's time for his preacher's collar to be replaced by a pair of .44s. But he won't be able to do it alone. If he's going to rid the town of this ruthless evil, he'll need to call on a very special group of warriors—the Sons of Thunder!

----

# LANCASTER'S ORPHANS
## Robert J. Randisi

It certainly isn't what Lancaster had expected. When he rode into Council Bluffs, he thought he would just stop at the bar for a beer. How could he know he'd ride right into the middle of a lynching? Lancaster can't let an innocent man be hanged, but when the smoke clears and the lynching stops, a bystander lies dying on the ground, caught in the crossfire. With his last breath he asks Lancaster to take care of the people who had been depending on him—a wagon train filled with women and children on their way to California!

---